# Empire Be
# The Fall of Sejanus

An Artorian Novella

# James Mace

Legionary Books
Meridian, Idaho 83642
http://www.legionarybooks.net

First eBook Edition: 2013

Published in the United States of America
Legionary Books

# The Works of James Mace

**The Artorian Chronicles**
Soldier of Rome: The Legionary (Book One)
Soldier of Rome: The Sacrovir Revolt (Book Two)
Soldier of Rome: Heir to Rebellion (Book Three)
Soldier of Rome: The Centurion (Book Four)
Soldier of Rome: Journey to Judea (Book Five)
Soldier of Rome: The Last Campaign (Book Six)

**Other Works**
I Stood With Wellington
Forlorn Hope: The Storming of Badajoz
Centurion Valens and the Empress of Death
Empire Betrayed: The Fall of Sejanus

*"You shoulder much, but do not take on yourself the evils committed by others."*

- Adela Theodora

# Background on the Character of
# Tribune Aulus Nautius Cursor

When I write characters into my stories, it is common for them to over time take on certain personality traits of people I know. This is natural, as it adds depth and realism, while making the characters relatable to readers. What is less common for me is to specifically create a character with the same appearance and personality of a friend or acquaintance. Tribune Cursor was the first time I wrote someone into the *Soldier of Rome* anthology specifically as a tribute to a friend.

To best understand Tribune Cursor, one should look at the man he is based on; retired U.S. Army Captain Jim Philpott. A Staff Sergeant when we first met, he spent twelve of his twenty years in the Army and Army National Guard as an enlisted Soldier. We served together in the same M1A1 tank company, and although we were never on the same crew, he was one who I always viewed as a mentor. After he commissioned, and while serving as a platoon leader, I myself had risen to Staff Sergeant and was one of his tank commanders. And while we clashed on occasion (*"Sir, I disagree"* was a phrase he dreaded hearing from me), an inseparable bond was formed between us, as well as our platoon sergeant, Ronald "Red" Oldham, and the other tank commander, Mike Smith. Of interesting note, Red substantially inspired the character of Centurion Platorius Macro in *The Artorian Chronicles*, and Mike provided the basis for Centurion Valerius Proculus, who returns in this story.

When I decided that I needed a cavalry officer in the fourth Artorian novel, *Soldier of Rome: The Centurion*, I could think of no one better to base this character on than Captain Jim Philpott. In addition to being a modern-day cavalry officer, Jim is also an avid runner. When I was searching for suitable Roman names, I came across the agnomen, *Cursor*, which literally means 'runner'. The name was perfect, and Aulus Nautius Cursor was born. He had a small role in a previous book, *Soldier of Rome: Heir to Rebellion*, prior to his leading of the 'charge of the ten thousand' in *The Centurion*. I do wish I had created the character earlier, because he could have played a substantial role in the first two books of the series.

As for this particular novella, it was originally supposed to be part of the background story for the fifth Artorian novel, *Soldier of Rome: Journey to Judea*. Because the fall of Sejanus and the brutal aftermath was such a traumatic series of events, it quickly became a distraction from the main story arc. I felt that it was something worth telling, and could stand on its own as a novella. And so, I cut all the scenes involving Sejanus' downfall and built this story around them. A lot of the details are sketchy in the primary sources, and so I've had to fill in the gaps using a lot of guesswork and no small amount of artistic license. And while characters are a refraction of the people we base them on, rather than a direct reflection, many of Tribune Cursor's traits correlate with Jim Philpott, in particular his sense of duty and an understanding that doing what is right often comes at a high price.

*James Mace – April* 2013

*Captain Jim Philpott and Tribune Aulus Nautius Cursor*

# Table of Contents

# Preface

In 29 A.D., Emperor Tiberius Caesar, living in self-imposed exile on the Isle of Capri, entrusts his Praetorian Prefect, Lucius Aelius Sejanus, with the administration of the vast Roman Empire. Under Sejanus' iron fist, and unbeknownst to Tiberius, the ranks of the Senate and equites are subsequently purged of the Praetorian's enemies. Treason trials, once prohibited in Rome, have become commonplace as Sejanus relentlessly punishes any who would defy him in his quest for power.

After many years of commanding the cavalry of the Army of the Rhine, Tribune Aulus Nautius Cursor at last returns to Rome, amidst the turmoil. Two years later is elected as a Tribune of the Plebs; the representatives of the people who hold the power of veto over the Senate. It is Cursor who discovers Sejanus' sinister plans; that he seeks to overthrow Tiberius and name himself Emperor.

Duty bound to save the Empire from falling further under a tyrannical usurper, Cursor resolves to unravel the conspiracy and bring the perpetrators to justice. Aiding him is an old friend; a retired Master Centurion named Gaius Calvinus. Regrettably, they know that if successful, Tiberius' retribution will be swift and brutal, sparing neither the innocent nor the guilty. This leaves only two dark paths for Cursor and Calvinus; either allow the pending reign of terror under a ruthless usurper, or unleash the unholy vengeance of an Emperor betrayed.

## Cast of Characters:

**Aulus Nautius Cursor** – Tribune of the Plebs, he is also a former cavalry officer who once saved an entire legion during the Battle of Braduhenna, four years prior

**Adela Theodora** – Wife of Cursor

**Gaius Calvinus** – A retired Master Centurion and now a fellow Tribune and friend of Cursor

**Lucius Aelius Sejanus** – Prefect of the Praetorian Guard, he is also the Emperor's most trusted advisor

**Naevius Suetorius Macro** – A driven, though morally questionable Praetorian, who will side with whomever necessary to achieve his ambitions

**Valerius Proculus, Tiberius Draco** – Retired senior-ranking Centurions, they now perform shadowy tasks for their friend, Calvinus

## Noble Romans:

**Tiberius Julius Caesar** – Emperor of Rome, living in self-imposed exile on the Isle of Capri, this allows Sejanus to rule in his absence

**Antonia** – Widow of the Emperor's brother, Drusus Nero, and also one of his only true friends

**Claudius** – Nephew of Tiberius, son of Antonia

**Livilla** – Daughter of Antonia, widow of Tiberius' son, Drusus Caesar

**Gaius Caligula** – Great-nephew of Tiberius, nephew of Claudius and Livilla through their late brother, Germanicus Caesar

# Chapter I: All Roads to Rome

*Rome*
*August, 29 A.D.*
***

The sun had just started to break over the hills to the east as the Eternal City came into view. The well-worn road the small group travelled on was known as the *Via Aurelia*, or *Aurelian Way*. It was nearly three hundred years old and served as the main thoroughfare from Rome to the west coast of Italia. At the head of the entourage rode a man dressed in a Tribune's armor, complete with muscled breastplate, with white leather trappings, a dark red cloak, and an ornate helmet, decorated with a lion's head on the crown and with a magnificent red crest running front-to-back. Far from being just ceremonial, his armor had seen battle on many occasions, and even constant polishing and buffing could not eliminate the scouring from the blows of countless enemy weapons.

His name was Aulus Nautius Cursor. Taller than most men, he had a pronounced nose that was common among many of the nobility, though it was devoid of the aquiline hook. His frame was lean and more designed for speed and agility, rather than brute power. Having gone completely bald at a young age, the padded skull cap beneath his helmet was doubly important. Now in his late thirties, he'd spent nearly twenty years as a military Tribune with the Army of the Rhine; substantially longer than many of his peers. All members of the lesser-nobles of the Roman Empire, known as the

*Equites*, were required to perform a minimum of six months with the legions. Though many stayed on longer than the compulsory time required, especially if other political or magisterial postings proved scarce, few ever made the army their primary career path. Being neither legionaries from the ranks, nor with ever having any opportunity to command legions as legates, Tribunes were confined to mostly staff duties. If one were lucky, he'd get command of a cohort of auxiliaries; the non-citizens who augmented the Roman Army with the promise of being awarded citizenship after twenty-five years of service.

For Cursor, his path had been much different. Though his name literally meant 'runner', and he was indeed quite nimble and fast on his feet, his true skill lay in horsemanship. His riding skills, plus natural ability for coordinating large bodies of fighting men, led to his assignment as a cavalry officer, under the tutelage of the now-legendary Commander Julius Indus. He'd also done his mandatory time as a staff officer, and was fortunate enough to have served directly under the late great, Germanicus Caesar. During the wars against the Germanic Alliance, following the disastrous ambush in Teutoburger Wald, Germanicus had demanded that all of his officers would first and foremost lead their men by their own example. In one of the few times he ever fought on foot, Cursor had accompanied his commanding general during the assault on a barbarian stronghold at Angrivarii; a terrible battle which thankfully brought the wars to an end.

Despite the accolades given to him for his bravery at Angrivarii, it was with the cavalry that the Tribune excelled, and it was following a rebellion in Gaul that he was given command of all mounted forces within the Rhine army. This was expanded even further during the Frisian Rebellion, when Cursor was handed operational control over all auxiliary forces during the campaign. With a force of ten thousand men, he had more soldiers under his charge than even the senatorial Legates who commanded the legions. It was at the Battle of Braduhenna that Cursor achieved his greatest glory, though he personally viewed it as his utmost tragedy.

"We've been away for far too long," his wife, Adela Theodora, said as the city came into view over the horizon. The River Tiber stretched before them, running north to south. Just beyond was the

Campus Martius, also known as the *Field of Mars*. A plethora of foreign temples and cults were housed here, as it also served as a place to greet dignitaries who could not for cultural reasons pass into the city proper. The most dominating feature of this district was the massive *Baths of Agrippa*. Beyond the field was the Capitoline; one of the famous Seven Hills that dominated Rome. The magnificent Temple of Jupiter rose from atop this hill and accented the skyline.

"To be honest, my love," Cursor replied, "It was on the Rhine, leading my regiments, that I felt most alive."

"And if you were still there, we should remain unmarried," his wife replied.

"Ours was indeed an unusual courtship," Cursor chuckled. Though arranged in the traditional sense by contract between Cursor and Adela's father, Theodorus, Adela herself had adamantly refused to follow through with the marriage as long as Cursor was still leading men into battle.

"Father relented once he saw that I would not budge, and that you were willing to wait for me." She had three sisters, two of whom had been widowed within their first couple years of marriage, when their husbands were killed in battle. The eldest had been wed to the Chief Tribune of the Twentieth Legion; in what their father felt was a great step forward, joining their family to the Senatorial class. Sadly, the young man was killed at Braduhenna, just four months into the marriage. He had never known that his wife was with child, though her grief would be compounded when their son was stillborn.

During what became a lengthy betrothal, Adela and her husband-to-be grew surprisingly close to each other. She had lived with family friends who owned an estate outside of Cologne, on the Rhine frontier. She therefore was able to remain close to Cursor, and was exceedingly proud of his valiant service to the Empire. However, she would not allow herself to become widowed like her sisters.

"Your father once told me that you were too intimidating for him to try and marry off to anyone else," Cursor remembered with a laugh. "He told me I'd better not die in battle; otherwise he wouldn't know what to do with you!" Adela simply smiled and shrugged. Being very statuesque, she was tall enough to easily look her husband in the eye, something that most normal-sized men found rather unnerving. Because Cursor treated her as an equal, their presence together made them a very strong couple.

As they reached the edge of the city, the streets were crowded with pedestrians, and they were compelled to dismount and lead their horses through the hectic thoroughfare, their travelling companions going their own ways. They skirted through a residential district, just north of the busy heart of the city. To the south was the Forum of Augustus; a small complex that housed the Temple of Mars Ultor. Further south, the great Capitoline Hill stood against the sky, with the Temple of Jupiter casting its shadow over the Roman Forum. As the road they were traveling along was crammed with street performers and observers, Cursor and Adela decided to chance going down a side street that would take them by Capitoline Hill and the Forum. Just before the Temple of Jupiter was the smaller Temple of Concord that overlooked the Forum itself.

"The Gemonian Stairs," Cursor observed, nodding towards the long steps that led up to the temple.

"The Stairs of Mourning," Adela added somberly. "Many a life has ended on those bloody steps."

One would never guess from the flocks of people climbing the steps that it served as the primary place of execution for notorious criminals. Almost inconspicuously off to the right of the Temple of Concord stood the Tullianum, a prison that was used to temporarily house those awaiting trial or execution. Interestingly enough, long-term prison sentences were rare in Roman society. Punishments such as public scourging or financial penalties sufficed for minor offenses, with banishment, enslavement, or death awaiting those found guilty of capital crimes. If one looked closely, they could almost see the blackened stains on the lower steps, where the bodies of the condemned were torn to pieces by the mob. As public executions were the norm in most parts of the world, both within and outside of the Empire, and that those who met their ignominious ends on the Gemonian Stairs hardly warranted pity, Cursor and Adela paid it no more mind and continued on their way.

On the outskirts of the Forum, Cursor saw the first face he had recognized all day. The man was in his early fifties, with close-cropped hair that was a mix of black and gray. He wore a formal toga, accented with the narrow purple stripe that identified him as a member of the Equites, though he carried himself with a force of authority, like an old soldier.

"By the gods," Cursor said with a grin, then hailing the man, "Calvinus!"

The man was startled for a moment at the call of his name, but broke into a broad grin as he walked over to Cursor and Adela. He instinctively almost saluted, but after a moment's pause extended his hand instead.

"Tribune, sir," he said.

"Please," Cursor replied, clasping the old soldier's hand, "I see by the purple stripe on your toga that you are now my peer. There is no need to call me 'sir'."

"Old habits," Calvinus replied with a nonchalant shrug. He then gave a respectful nod towards the Tribune's wife. "Lady Adela."

"A pleasure," she replied. "I don't believe we've met."

"Gaius Calvinus, ma'am; I served with the Twentieth Legion when your husband commanded the cavalry of the Rhine Army."

"And as a retired Master Centurion, he was elevated into the Equites," Cursor added.

"Rome does afford at least some opportunities to better one's social standing," Calvinus observed, "If one has the ambition to use them."

"I did not know you returned to Rome," Cursor said.

"My daughter and her family live in Neapolis," Calvinus explained, walking with them and helping guide their way through the Forum. "This brought me close enough that I can at least pay them the occasional visit. It was bad enough that Calvina grew up hardly knowing her father, and with my grandson fast approaching manhood, I felt compelled to make up for lost time. And besides, how many retired soldiers have the opportunity to influence the governing of our beloved Empire after they remove their armor for the last time?"

"Very few," Cursor conceded. For every hundred men who served out their term in the legions, perhaps three or four would be in a position to have a second career in continuing service to Rome. And only approximately three in every thousand ever achieved sufficient rank to elevate themselves up the social ladder.

"I felt a responsibility that once I was officially named an Equite, I needed to act as a voice for our brethren still in the ranks. I have no desire to try for a governorship or anything of that nature. However, it would be unethical if I took the privileges of being raised up within the social orders and not any of the responsibilities. If I can still be of service to Rome, I will."

Roman society was extremely rigid in its class structure, with every citizen and non-citizen expected to know their place without question. Those within the Senatorial class were the noble patricians who lorded over the Empire, answerable only to the Emperor. All were from the oldest and wealthiest families within Rome, and while at any time as many as three hundred were sitting members of the Senate, their total number was perhaps six hundred to a thousand total households.

The Equites were the lesser nobles who provided the Empire with many of its magistrates, public officials, minor provincial governors, as well as military Tribunes and the coveted Tribunes of the Plebs. Those not born into this class could be elevated into it by serving in the army; though this often required one attaining the rank of Centurion Primus Pilus, also known as a *Master Centurion*. Centurions who had served as cohort commanders were also sometimes eligible. As soldiers who retired at these exalted ranks were so few in number, they made up a very small fraction of this class. All told, there were perhaps a few thousand members of the Equites, and between them and the Senate they made up the noble classes of an Empire that numbered around seventy million persons.

"Where will you be staying?" Calvinus asked as they skirted the Forum and passed the Temple of the Divine Romulus, at the start of the street known as the *Via Sacra*, or *Sacred Way*.

"I arranged purchase of a house not too far from here," Cursor said, "Thankfully it keeps us away from the daily insanity of the Forum. We're about a mile south of the Castra Praetoria." The place he referred to was the central barracks of the Emperor's Praetorian Guard.

"Ah, I'm not far from you at all," Calvinus observed. "Well I have to be off again; remember, I have not been away from the legions for long and am still learning the ways of an Equite former soldier who still wishes to serve the public. Give yourself a day or two to get settled, and then please call upon us. Lady Adela, my wife, Petronia, would love to make your acquaintance."

"Likewise," Adela replied. As they watched the old soldier make this way through the crowds, she turned to her husband. "Did you know him well?"

"Well enough," Cursor replied. "He was one of the few survivors of that disastrous ambush in Teutoburger Wald, twenty years ago. He and a young Tribune named Cassius Chaerea saved the lives of over a hundred legionaries when they cut their way out of that nightmare. It was also his legion that my men trekked forty miles in a day to relieve after they were cut off and surrounded at Braduhenna."

As wheeled traffic was only permitted on the streets of Rome at night, it was well after midnight by the time the wagons bearing Cursor and Adela's baggage arrived at their house. They'd had the good sense to send servants a day or two ahead of them to purchase a suitable bed and a few other immediate necessities. Adela decided to pass the time with a lengthy bath. One amenity they had that most of the general populace did not was the privilege of having one's own private bath, rather than having to use those crowded public facilities scattered throughout the city. Having her skin scraped and oiled by a servant, she lounged in the heated waters of the hot bath and allowed herself to drift off.

She was uncertain how much time had passed when she roused herself from her plunge. Her maidservant was waiting with fresh robes, and after dressing, Adela made her way up the dark flight of stairs to their suite. The household staff was still unloading baggage, though she paid them little mind. She expected her husband would have been in bed by this late hour; however, she could see the faint glow of light coming from the room that would be his private study.

Curious, Adela walked noiselessly down the short hallway to where the door was barely cracked open. Inside, Cursor stood over a table, an oak box lying open on top. In his hands he held a crude circlet of grass and weeds, held together by hardened mud. Though it looked more like something a ragged barbarian would wear, and contrasting sharply with any form of Roman décor, it was in fact Rome's most prestigious award for valor, and Aulus Cursor was the only currently living recipient in the whole of the Empire. His eyes were shut, his head bowed in deep thought…

*"Make ready to storm the gates of hell…charge of the ten thousand!"* The Tribune's voice was breaking as he salvaged what was left of his strength for one final assault. He could not remember the last time he'd slept; and since the previous afternoon, he and his men had trekked twenty miles up the River Rhine, crossed, and then back again. The forced march through the black of night, unable to see or hear anything except the raging river for endless hours, without knowing if his men were even still with him, had nearly driven him completely mad. He was beyond exhausted; all of his senses were numb.

His cavalry regiments formed the center of a massive wedge, with infantry cohorts on the flanks. The Tribune had instinctively placed himself at the apex of the wedge, knowing that if he were first into the fray, his men would follow. At this point, he reasoned that if he did fall, death would be a reprieve from his utter exhaustion and pain.

The Frisian army was huge; they had managed to trap an entire legion with its back to the Rhine. The legionaries had been in a desperate fight for their lives since the previous afternoon, and the Tribune did not know if any of them were even still alive. The Frisians were devoid of armor, with most carrying small board or wicker shields, with hand axes, clubs, or stabbing spears for weapons. A small number of the wealthier warriors carried swords, either Roman-style gladii, or great broadswords. What they lacked in protection and armament they made up for in overwhelming numbers, discipline, and extreme courage.

Many of the enemy warriors had been caught by surprise as the wall of men and horses crashed into them, with many being toppled and cut down in the onslaught. The Tribune watched as his long spatha cavalry sword smashed into the skull of one such man with a loud snap, cutting deep into the brain and mercifully killing the warrior instantly. He lost all sense of awareness to his surroundings; he was now in a battle for his life, as were the rest of his men who crashed into the flank of the Frisian army. His horse reared up as a spear was brandished in its face, almost throwing its rider off. The Tribune gripped the reins tightly and spun the beast about, allowing him to thrust his sword deep into his assailant's throat. The man's eyes bulged and his tongue stuck grotesquely between his teeth as

18

blood erupted from this throat and mouth. Unable to hear anything over the roar of clashing arms and the screams of wounded men and horses, the Tribune realized that their charge was foundering. The Frisian numbers were too great, and the complete fatigue of his men was quickly proving to be their undoing.

Then out of the corner of his eye he saw the flash of red shields. Large formations of legionaries were assembling to the right of his force, unleashing storms of javelins into their hapless foes. These were not the cut off remnants of the Twentieth who had been cut off this entire time; these men were from the Fifth Legion, who had spent the entire night rebuilding the severed bridges across the Rhine. They were mostly fresh, and were smashing into the Frisians with a vengeance.

His senses still numb, the Tribune signaled for his nearest cavalry regiments to follow him. They quickly pulled back away from the harrowing battle, as the Frisians were attempting to face this renewed onslaught of legionaries. The Tribune knew that the shock of his charge, which had driven their enemy away from the bridges and given the Fifth room to cross, combined with a flanking assault by five thousand relatively fresh legionaries, would break them soon enough. His intent now was to maneuver his cavalry around the flank and behind the enemy. His auxiliary infantry and remaining cavalry regiments continued to gallantly hold their ground as cohorts of legionaries formed up to reinforce them with alarming speed and discipline; each century unleashing its javelins before drawing their gladii and charging into the hell storm of men and metal.

As his horsemen made their way around to the rear of the barbarian force, the Tribune caught sight of the only enemy mounted troops on the field. It was the Frisian king himself! Though his bodyguard could have easily held the Roman cavalry long enough for the king to escape, his sword was drawn and he was leading his men in their final charge. As the Tribune ordered his men to reform and attack, he was struck with a sense of admiration for the Frisian king's selfless courage; that he was willing to die with his warriors.

The king's household cavalry was badly outnumbered and outmatched by the Roman horsemen, and the entire clash, spectacular as it was, was over in a minute. The ranking Centurion who accompanied the Tribune, who was ironically a Frisian by birth, was the one who cut down the enemy king. He unhorsed him with a

19

hard slash across the body and flaying his guts open as the king fell hard to the earth, his stricken horse landing on top of him. His vision clouded, the Tribune now had difficulty focusing on the ongoing battle, where the enemy army's flank had collapsed and a panic was running amok amongst the warriors. Pursuit would prove impossible, for the Tribune had the only Roman cavalry on this side of the Rhine, and both men and horse were completely spent. The soldiers of the Fifth Legion would not be able to mount any sort of effective chase, encumbered as they were by their heavy armor and weapons. But for them, there was the euphoria and relief that came from knowing that where once all was lost, the battle had now been won.

The Tribune caught his first glance of the wreckage of the Twentieth Legion, and was surprised to see that any of them were still alive. Though many were dead or seriously wounded, the majority of the legionaries still stood, completely spent but defiant. Those who'd taken it the worst was a lone century that had held the extreme flank. Few of these men could stand, and the small patch of ground was littered with bodies, both Frisian and Roman. The Tribune almost collapsed as he quickly dismounted upon seeing the unit's Centurion lying on the ground, his hand clasped over a deep gash in his side, where his armor had been ruptured. His smashed helmet lay several feet away, and he was bleeding from a nasty gash behind his ear from where his helm had been ripped from his head. The man, whose name was Artorius, was someone the Tribune had always considered a friend, despite his status as a plebian soldier from the ranks. The two clasped hands, though neither would remember what words had passed between them.

The Tribune's next memory came from later that afternoon. The survivors of the Twentieth Legion, still looking battered and filthy, were standing in formation. In a reversal of protocol, all officers stood at the back. Posted in front of the mass of legionaries was a young soldier, who appeared to be all of seventeen. In his hands was a crown made of grass and weeds, taken from the trampled field of battle. Though most awards presented to Roman soldiers were made of gold or silver, the two most prestigious came from the humble earth. The *Civic Crown*, awarded for saving the life of a fellow soldier or citizen, was made of oak leaves instead of gold, as it was reasoned that a gold crown would be putting a price on human life.

The crown held by the young legionary was of an even greater honor, and was for saving not just one life, but an entire legion. It was also the only award that was presented by the men in the ranks, by universal acclamation. It was so prestigious and rare that it had not been awarded to any soldier for at least a couple of generations.

"Tribune Aulus Nautius Cursor," the legionary spoke, "It is by your actions in leading your ten thousand forty miles in a single day, flanking the Frisian army, and killing the enemy King that you have saved the Valeria Legion from being wiped out of existence. It is by universal acclamation of the men of the Twentieth that we present you Rome's most sacred honor, the *Grass Crown*."

The Tribune removed his helmet, tucking it under his left arm, and bowed his head slightly as the legionary placed the crown on his bald head. The soldier then drew his gladius and turned to face the legion.

*"Twentieth Legion!"* he shouted. *"Gladius...draw!"*

*"Rah!"* responded the host of legionaries, who had been deathly silent to this point, as their weapons flew from their scabbards.

*"Salute!"*

*"Ave Cursor, savior of Valeria!"*

Adela's eyes grew wet as she watched her husband go through his somber ritual. Though the Battle of Braduhenna, which had taken place just east of the River Rhine, was a Roman victory, it was regarded as an unmitigated disaster. It was well known throughout the Empire that Cursor was awarded the Grass Crown, yet many of Rome's nobles resented him for it. It was viewed by some as dishonorable that the legionaries of the Twentieth Valeria had taken the initiative to honor him for saving their lives. Cursor had certainly never asked to be awarded for his actions, and in fact avoided any mentioning of what happened that dark day.

Soon after the ceremony, he had spoken with Centurion Artorius, who had watched from a distance, being unable to stand and wearing only a loin cloth and a large bandage over his badly injured side. Cursor had told the Centurion that it felt more like a crown of lead than of grass.

"It is a heavy burden you now bear," Artorius had replied. "But know that your place in history is well earned."

Whatever his thoughts were about the heavy burden the Grass Crown brought to him, he kept it with him as a sacred possession, in honor of those who died at Braduhenna. Adela watched as her husband took a small pitcher of water and lightly sprinkled a few drops over the crown to keep it moist and from becoming brittle. He then closed his eyes, placed the crown to his lips, and set it reverently back into its box. Adela watched for a moment longer as he closed the lid and bowed his head, eyes still closed. She had never seen him go through this ritual before, and wondered how often he performed it, or if this was the first time. What she did know, and it broke her heart to come to this understanding, was that the man she loved had had his very soul broken on that horrible battlefield, fighting in a terrible war that would later be regarded as unjustified; the magistrate who brought it about being personally executed by the Emperor himself. The hardest thing for Adela Theodora to accept was that the pain Cursor bore would always be there, and there was nothing she could do to ever ease it.

# Chapter II: Emperor in Exile

*Imperial Estate of Villa Jovis, Isle of Capri*
*30 September, 29 A.D.*

\*\*\*

*Emperor Tiberius Julius Caesar*

"So Livia has at last passed into the afterlife," Tiberius said as he read the scroll, handed to him by his Praetorian Prefect, Lucius Aelius Sejanus. For the last several years he'd referred to the Empress dowager by her given name, as if it somehow rendered meaningless the fact that she was his mother. For the Emperor Tiberius Julius Caesar, the news could not have come soon enough. The two had been estranged for years, and the very fact that she'd lived so long had been a constant thorn in his side.

"I thought I should convey the message to you personally," Sejanus replied, his face ever stoic. "September bears yet another somber date for the imperial family," he added humorlessly.

The month of September was always one of conflicting emotions for Tiberius. The 18th was the anniversary of his succession to the imperial throne, following the death of his stepfather, the Divine

23

Augustus, fifteen years prior. It was also in September, six years before, that Tiberius had lost his only son, Drusus Julius Caesar.

"Indeed," the Emperor acknowledged. Tiberius Julius Caesar Augustus, as he'd been known since his rise to the imperial throne, was certainly not a young man. At nearly seventy-one years of age, he'd outlived most of his peers. Given that his mother had just passed into eternity, his was a long-lived line. In his younger years, he was certain that he'd be killed in battle, and as such fought with valor that bordered on recklessness, showing utter contempt for his own safety. He mentioned this to his Prefect, whose expression remained unchanged.

"The gods had other plans for you, Caesar," he replied smoothly. Tiberius snorted in reply, but Sejanus continued, "Surely they saw your abilities, not just leading men into battle, but knowing when to draw the sword and when to use the weapon of diplomacy."

"You refer to my little foray into the east," Tiberius noted, squinting his eyes as he looked back into his remote past. "By Juno, it's been almost forty years since I led the legions into Armenia! Not many remember that anymore."

"I remember it," the Prefect observed. "I was just a boy of ten or eleven then, but I do remember the glorious return of a young Legate, restoring with honor the Roman standards lost decades before to the Parthians by Crassus, Sexta, and Marc Antony."

"Antony's debacle with the Parthians was overshadowed by his affair with Cleopatra and subsequent defeat by Octavian a few years later," Tiberius said with a chuckle. "Even I have long forgotten many of those days. I often wonder if I am even the same person who not only compelled the Parthians to return the lost standards, but to also respect Armenia's independence as a neutral and sovereign nation that has since acted as a buffer between our Empires."

"And you did it without shedding a drop of Roman blood," Sejanus added.

"My next campaigns were not so clean," Tiberius stated, seeming to enjoy the momentary distraction of long-lost memories. "It took months to return from Armenia, and no sooner had I arrived than Augustus sent me and my brother north and west."

"The conquest of the Alpes," Sejanus said. "And the crushing of the barbarians in Transalpine Gaul, as well as the conquest of Raetia."

"I'll tell you, Sejanus; those were the best years of my life. I spent thirteen years fighting in Augustus' wars, expanding and consolidating the Empire. I fought in many battles, saw friends die, and I have more scars than I can count. Yet for all that, I *believed* in what I was doing! I was also married to the only woman I ever loved, and when she gave me my son, my life truly was complete…by the gods, what happened to me?" His face darkened, and his short reprieve of good humor vanished, leaving in its wake the perpetual gloom he was notorious for. He then brandished the scroll bearing the news of his mother's death, his face hard with rage. "*She* did this to me!"

"I should take my leave, Caesar," Sejanus replied calmly as Tiberius threw the scroll across the room.

"No," the Emperor said quickly waving his hand. "Forgive me, my friend. You understand how little I have left in this world. I once loved my mother; I wished more than anything to please her. I never faulted her for divorcing my father and marrying Octavian. The irony was that my father actually gave her away at her wedding! She may have been intuitive and knew that the Republic was gasping its last breath, but even she could not have known that Octavian would eventually become Augustus Caesar, Emperor of Rome."

"There was respect between you and Augustus," Sejanus observed.

"Perhaps," Tiberius said begrudgingly, "But never love. Once I was old enough, he sent me to fight in his wars, arranged my marriage to the daughter of his best friend, and when that was no longer politically of use, forced me to divorce her so I could marry his bitch of a daughter, Julia. I was a weapon to be used at his disposal like a gladius or javelin, nothing more. I think we only really began to understand each other when he was in his final days. I look back on those who had the most profound impact on my life; Augustus, Livia, Vipsania, my dear brother, my son…but they are gone now, all of them. You, the partner of my labors, are all I have left."

Tiberius dismissed Sejanus and took a walk along the cliff face that his palace sat atop of. The island itself was heavily forested, with thick groves of trees lining all of the roads both in and out of the towns. Looking straight down the rocky cliffs, the water of the

Mediterranean was a deep blue, accented by the shimmering light of the early evening sun that was beginning its descent into the west. Despite years on the frontier, and all the injuries suffered in numerous conflicts, the Emperor had never succumbed to the effects of fatigue and age until the death of his son. In that instant, Tiberius Caesar became an old man. For all his faults, Drusus had been his last bastion of light in the blackness that now enveloped his soul.

"I could have saved you from yourself," he said quietly, hoping that perhaps in the afterlife his son could hear him. Drusus had lived a hard life of self-indulgence and drink. His best friend was a Judean prince named Herod Agrippa, who had been sent to Rome as a young boy and Tiberius had raised as if he were his own son. Agrippa blamed himself for Drusus' premature death. He was ill for months and ceased most of his drinking, yet it had been far too late. Though he was only thirty-six at the time of his death, his poor health and hazardous lifestyle led few to question his demise.

Not long prior, Drusus had had a nasty quarrel with Sejanus, whom he despised immensely. The imperial prince had even struck the Praetorian Prefect, though Sejanus refused to raise a hand to defend himself. He would later say that in his weakened health, Drusus was not in a right state of mind, and was so enfeebled that an old woman could have overpowered him. A month later, Drusus Julius Caesar was dead.

"I am supposed to protect an Empire, yet I could not even save my own son," Tiberius continued as the warm breeze off the sea blew against his face, ruffling the folds of his toga. "Please forgive me." Tears no longer came to the Emperor. He had suffered so much loss in his life, that his very soul had become hard as stone. And with his mother's long-anticipated death, every person of significance in Tiberius' life was now gone. His father had died when he was still a boy; his brother, Drusus Nero--who Tiberius had named his son in honor of--had perished following a bad riding accident at the age of twenty-nine.

And yet there was one who he missed more than all others combined. Though compelled by Augustus to divorce his wife, Vipsania, who later remarried one of his most hated rivals, Tiberius had never ceased loving her. She had died of a mysterious illness nearly ten years prior, while still only in her fifties. Her feelings must have been the same, for when he saw her just before her death, her last words to him were, *'I will wait for you'*. He clung to those words, like a drowning man to a floating branch.

It was a bit of an exaggeration for Tiberius to say that he was completely alone. There were a few family members still alive, though he lacked the feelings of affection he'd held for his wife, son, and even his mother at one time. His brother's widow, Antonia, who surprisingly never remarried, was probably his closest true friend. Her eldest son, Germanicus Caesar, had been one of Rome's greatest generals and was at one time named as Tiberius' successor. Antonia and Drusus Nero's daughter, Livilla, had been married to her cousin, Tiberius' son, Drusus Caesar, and the Emperor was still very fond of her. Sejanus had at one time asked for permission to marry her, but as this had been only a couple years after Drusus' death, and the backlash of gossips speaking of the Praetorian Prefect trying to marry his way into the imperial family, Tiberius had denied his request.

Drusus did leave behind a son and daughter, though they were still very young, lived with their mother, and the Emperor never saw them. That left his other nephew, Antonia's youngest son, Claudius. As the brother of Germanicus, and with no other realistic bloodline heirs, there were some in the Senate who'd pushed for Claudius to be proclaimed as Tiberius' heir. But as he was a complete imbecile who stammered and had an annoying nervous twitch, the Emperor had immediately crushed any such notions. As he put it, even the benevolent Augustus had done everything to keep the embarrassing Claudius out of the public eye.

It was with no small trace of irony that the Emperor's nephew, Claudius, elected to pay him a visit on Capri a few days after Livia's death. Sejanus, who was set to return to Rome with some official dispatches from the Emperor, had remained on the island just long enough to greet him.

"Hail, brother!" he said with a broad grin as servants opened the large doors leading in the main foyer. He knew Claudius hated it when he addressed him so, yet with Sejanus arranging the marriage between his sister, Aelia, and the young man, he was well within his rights. In a further show of faux affection that would grate on Claudius, Sejanus embraced him hard.

"A…and good to see you too," Claudius said, his voice ever choppy. He did his best to suppress his stammer around his brother-in-law, yet for whatever reason it usually worsened.

"I take it my sister is well?"

"W…well enough," Claudius replied. "You c…could always pay her a visit. You know she is with child."

"Yes, so I heard," Sejanus replied almost dismissively. "Well, I only hope that the babe takes on certain qualities of its mother." The thinly veiled insult, referring to Claudius' limp and speech impediments, was not lost on him.

"What surprises me," Claudius replied, regaining control over his stammer, "Is that it was you who p…pressed me into marrying Aelia. And yet your rapport with me has been one of n…near contempt."

"No, you misjudge me, brother," the Praetorian said, placing a friendly hand on his shoulder.

"Well, I came to pay my respects to my uncle," Claudius said as he walked slowly towards the stairs that led up to the Emperor's study on the second floor.

"Yes, I'm sure he'll be thrilled to see you," Sejanus replied, not moving. His next words stopped Claudius in his tracks. "You know there's been talk in certain quarters about you being named as Tiberius' successor."

Claudius turned back and tried to sound dismissive, though it was clear Sejanus' words had struck him hard. "Tiberius would not even let me begin the *cursus honorum*, and has never so much as allowed me to stand for public office. I t…think he is more likely to name *you* his successor than me." He quickly turned back and started his slow trek up the flight of stairs.

Sejanus chuckled quietly to himself. As he left the Villa Jovis, he was joined by a Senator named Julius Silvanus. Being of the old Julian line, Silvanus hated Tiberius and the Claudian family that had surpassed their dominance of Rome.

"Think your brother-in-law will pose a threat to us?" Silvanus asked candidly.

"Claudius is not the fool he pretends to be," Sejanus noted. "And whatever animosity he may garner from the imperial family, the people love him."

"Love him like a handicapped child or broken dog," the Senator scoffed.

"Regardless, Claudius is no threat to us. That love from the public, whatever its origins or motives, combined with his marriage to my sister, will serve us well."

"A rather coy move that was," Silvanus chuckled, "Convincing him to divorce his first wife, as she was pregnant with another man's child; only to find that she was also implicated in a murder! You further grant him a 'favor' by offering up your own sister as his new bride, thereby affiliating yourself with the imperial house. Well, it's not the marriage to Livilla that you wanted, but it'll suffice."

"My proposed marriage to Livilla was not just about political maneuvering," Sejanus replied with ice in his voice.

"Of course, I meant no offense." Silvanus knew Sejanus' potential for taking down political rivals. Indeed he had helped the Praetorian try, convict, and dispatch of more than a few Senators who had meddled in his affairs one-too-many times. As the Julians were Sejanus' closest allies, and Silvanus had been among his staunchest supporters, his own position was relatively secure. However, he did not wish to incur Sejanus' wrath when concerning the woman he professed to love.

"Livilla was once destined to be Empress of Rome," the Praetorian further emphasized, "And Empress she shall be!"

"Before we move too much further, let us not forget one rival we need to strike down very soon."

"Yes," Sejanus replied, his voice calm and calculated once more. "And fortunately for us, this man is such a hated rival of Tiberius' that he will be all too pleased for us to help rid the Empire of him."

Claudius' call to pay respects to his uncle had been an awkward meeting to say the least. The two had never been close. Though Tiberius said repeatedly that his brother was one of the only people he ever loved, those feelings did not extend to his brother's last surviving son.

Claudius made note of this to Asinius Gallus, the Senator at whose house he dined several days later. Gallus, whose contemptible hatred for the Emperor was no secret, simply scoffed at the remark.

"Tiberius would strike down members of his own family as readily as anyone else," the old Senator remarked. "You know I never absolved him of guilt in the death of your brother, and I sometimes think that you being married to Sejanus' sister is what keeps you safe, my friend."

Gallus was close in age to the Emperor, having served as Consul nearly forty years prior. Two of his sons had also risen through the Senatorial ranks and had been elected to terms as Consul, much to the chagrin of Tiberius. Gallus' father, Asinius Pollio, had been a prominent soldier, scholar, and historian, whose works Claudius read voraciously as a boy.

"I c...confess I am surprised he has not lashed out against you," Claudius thought aloud.

"There are days I take a certain amount of pleasure in being his most hated rival," Gallus mused. "I married the only woman he ever loved, yet who he was forced to spurn so that he could eventually assume the imperial mantle." Tiberius' former wife, Vipsania, had married Gallus not long after their divorce. That the man who never ceased to profess his love for her had cast her off simply because Augustus told him to had left her feeling betrayed and vulnerable.

"T...there was rumor that it was you who fathered Drusus and not my uncle," Claudius said awkwardly.

"No worries, lad, it wasn't true," Gallus reassured him. "I never so much as paid a second glance to Vipsania until after Tiberius had no more use for her. I only allowed the gossip to persist because I knew it would make his blood boil. You know I was very fond of Augustus, despite his ending of the Republic. Even though my father remained steadfastly neutral during the civil war between him and Antony, he still later gave him much in the way of public funding for his great library and other works."

"He did respect your father as a scholar," Claudius agreed.

"Tiberius, though, was about the worst successor Augustus could have chosen. The *father of our nation* left us with a totalitarian despot to rule after he'd gone." Over the years, Gallus opposed nearly every measure to come from Tiberius, and had become a sort of voice for the opposition.

As if his words had cued an ominous omen, there was a loud banging on the large doors leading into the outer atrium. Gallus stood as they heard a loud commotion once servants opened the door. The sound of several men marching in step with hobnailed sandals echoed in the large hall. In a moment, half a dozen Praetorian Guardsmen stepped into the dining hall. At their head was a Tribune who Claudius recognized.

"Cassius," Gallus said, his face full of tension, "A bit late to be calling. What is the meaning of this?"

"Asinius Gallus?" the Tribune asked, ignoring his words.

"Oh come of it, man, you know I am!"

"I have a warrant for your arrest...I am sorry." His last words were said quietly as he held up a small scroll.

"By whose order?" Gallus asked. "Certainly not the Emperor, he would not dare arrest me, hated rivals we may be!" The Tribune then handed him the scroll, and Gallus' face darkened as he saw the seal was not of Tiberius, but Sejanus. "I see."

"Take him," Cassius said to the Guardsmen who accompanied him. "And go easy on him, he's an old man!"

"Well Claudius," Gallus said, looking back to his guest, whose mouth was open in shock. "You will have to finish our dinner without me. It would seem your brother-in-law gains more control over the Empire every day. Hades knows who he will strike down next!"

Claudius stumbled to his feet, his natural limp, as well as a little too much wine, causing him to fall right into the Praetorian Tribune, Cassius Chaerea, who helped him upright himself.

"Take it easy, sir," he said consolingly as his men led Gallus out into the night.

"H...how can you allow this?" Claudius said, exacerbated. "Gallus may be the Emperor's r...rival, but he is no traitor. You know this!"

"That I do," Cassius agreed. "Believe me, I don't like this any more than you do."

"I must s...speak with my brother-in-law about this outrage!" Claudius made to move past the Tribune, who stopped him with a hand firmly on his chest. "By Juno, unhand me, sir!" He immediately regretted snapping. Cassius was both a national hero and one whom Claudius had immense respect for.

"Apologies," the Tribune replied calmly. "I only wish to keep you from doing anything rash. What possible good do you think it will do if you go to Sejanus? You may be married to his sister, but he views you as no brother. You were simply a means to an end for him, to connect him by marriage to the imperial family. And that is why you are still safe, because he needs that bond to legitimize his continuing grasp for power. He is setting things in motion to become Consul within a year, and by that point he may not need you anymore. Do nothing to antagonize him, but keep your wife close. You have a child coming, don't you?"

"Y…yes," Claudius said, his head twitching involuntarily.

"Then keep him…or her, close to you as well," Cassius remarked as he made to leave.

"And what will you do?"

"My duty," Cassius replied. "But do not mistake that to mean I will just blindly follow orders while a usurper rises."

# Chapter III: Broken Hero

*Rome*
*February, 31 A.D.*
***

Two years had now passed since Cursor's return to Rome. Several prominent magistrates had arranged for his appointment as a *Quaestor*. While the position did not involve the leading of military troops, it was an important posting that oversaw financial matters within Rome. Cursor had a knack for numbers and found that he actually enjoyed his work. With no costly wars being fought and the Empire focused on economic stability, rather than expansion, the imperial coffers had swelled considerably over the past few years.

One thing that troubled the Tribune was the perception that the demeanor of many of his colleagues was either condescending or else full of false flattery. Even those who had helped him gain his appointment had only done so as a means of furthering their own political career paths, by befriending a man who was regarded as a military hero, albeit a reluctant one. Much to their disappointment, Cursor was not one who would use his status as a Grass Crown recipient to further his own career, let alone someone else's. This had led to many fair-weather friends to suddenly become very cold and distant towards him.

The only man who seemed to share a genuine friendship with the Tribune was Gaius Calvinus. The retired Master Centurion had left the army not long after Braduhenna and he had over the last couple years become close with the Tribune whose cavalry charge had helped save his legion. Calvinus had been elected as a *Tribune of the Plebs* upon his return to Rome in an election that surprised many. Though still of a lower social class than the Senate, a man elected as a Plebian Tribune potentially held enormous power. During the Republic, they were considered to be the *voice of the people*, with the power to veto any laws or decrees passed by the Senate that the populace found to be unjust. Their persons were also considered to be absolutely inviolable. They required no bodyguard escort, for to harm one was not only a crime, it was considered a sacrilege against the gods that even the most black-hearted brigand would not dare offend. Cursor made mention of Calvinus' rather expedient election one afternoon as the two left a meeting at the Forum.

"It was a matter of timing, I suppose," Calvinus shrugged.

"Yes, but you had only just been elevated to the Equites upon your retirement from the legions," Cursor persisted. "Most will go their entire political careers without ever standing for, let alone becoming a Plebian Tribune."

"Well, the position doesn't quite mean what it once did," the former Master Centurion reasoned. "During the Republic, our power was vast. The Senate would court our favor, just to keep us from vetoing their favored legislation. While technically we can still veto the Senate, no one ever does. With the Emperor also holding the Tribunician authority, he can use the veto power himself; and his trumps ours. Therefore we do not dare exercise veto, in case the Senate passes a decree that the Emperor is in favor of. I'd hate to think what would happen to any poor sod that did! So as you can see, old friend, though my position is steeped in honor and tradition, it does not hold real power like it once did. You're in a far better position to accomplish something tangible as a Quaestor."

"You could always use the veto to override the sentences of some of these damn treason trials," Cursor lamented. "From what I have seen, none have been personally endorsed by Tiberius, except perhaps Asinius Gallus." Since his return to Rome, the Tribune had been appalled to see a number of Senators and other nobles of impeccable character and service suddenly brought before trial on charges of treason, often under outlandish circumstances. It was lost on no one that every last person brought before the courts was an enemy of Sejanus.

"An unwise decision," a voice said behind them. The two men turned to see Julius Silvanus looking down his nose at both of them.

"Senator," Calvinus said coldly.

"Do you always pry into other people's conversations?" Cursor added, matching the Senator's pompous gaze with a hard glare.

"Any conversations that could be construed as seditious are my concern, be they private or no," Silvanus sneered. He shifted his arm and shoulder to emphasize the broad purple stripe on his toga that signified him as a Senator, whereas Cursor and Calvinus only bore the narrow stripe of the Equites.

"Seditious?" Cursor said, turning to face him. "There was a time when the Emperor forbid bringing men to trial for the use of mere words, no matter how seditious or unsavory. *'In a free state there must be freedom of speech and thought,'* those were his words! Now people are being strangled and tossed into the Tiber over 'treasonable utterances'!"

"You forget yourself, *Equite*," Silvanus snarled. He then waved over at Calvinus. "Your friend's person may be inviolable while he holds his office, but yours is not! Those trials have been under the orders of Sejanus...*Consul* Sejanus, in case you've forgotten. So if you are smart, you'll mind your tongue." Before either Tribune could say another word, the Senator promptly left.

"Insufferable prick," Cursor growled, just loud enough that he hoped Silvanus could hear him.

"I hate to say it, but he's right about one thing," Calvinus remarked. "Times have changed, my friend. Rome is no longer a state of free speech and thought."

The door slammed open in Sejanus' study at the Praetorian barracks. Though he now held the Consulship jointly with Tiberius, he had kept his primary administrative offices at the Praetorium. The Prefect looked up from his desk, which was piled with documents, and raised an eyebrow.

"You seem vexed, Silvanus," he said with a bored sigh. "What is it this time; or rather *who* is it?"

"An insufferable Equite," Silvanus fumed. Sejanus merely raised an eyebrow, and the Senator immediately corrected himself. "Apologies; I know you were born of the same class, but the Emperor has seen fit to elevate you beyond the confines of the lesser nobles."

"Yes, and your own speech to the Senate, compelling them to vote against their better judgment to confirm my position as co-Consul with the Emperor was rather moving, albeit a bit overzealous on the threats. Still, you helped convince the Fathers of Rome to vote in favor of an appointment that was undeniably illegal. Now, what of this Equite? Who is he and what has he done to offend you?"

"His offense is trying to convince one the Plebian Tribunes to use his veto to override the courts. His name is Aulus Cursor; I'm sure you've heard of him."

"Everyone has heard of Aulus Cursor," Sejanus replied with no change in his demeanor, "Even if no one speaks of him. We'll keep an eye on him, but should not be too obsessive about bringing him down. He's the only living *Grass Crown* recipient of our time, and whether he knows it or not, that buys him a lot of protection. Even a constant nuisance can prove useful, my friend. Should he compel one of the Plebian Tribunes to use his power, it instills confidence in the public that the system still works; they need not know that with one word from me, the Emperor will override any Tribunician veto. But as he has caused you some offense, I think we can find a suitable means of slapping his hand." He held up a dispatch that bore the Emperor's seal.

"What have you there?" Silvanus asked.

"Just the latest message from our beloved Emperor," Sejanus answered with thick sarcasm. "Amongst his usual ramblings, he asks that I find a use for his great-nephew, Gaius Caligula. I think a certain Quaestor position will soon be vacant."

After the events of the day and the quarrel with Senator Silvanus, Cursor was unable to sleep. Adela found him in his study, a small oil lamp burning on the desk, his scabbarded cavalry sword lying in his lap. Called a *spatha*, it looked very similar to a legionary gladius, except for its much longer blade that was necessary when fighting from horseback. The leather scabbard was painted a very dark red; the brass fittings that the leather straps tied into were decorated with palm leaves, with a lion's head in the center, almost identical to the one that adorned the front of his Tribune's helm. The handle of the weapon itself was of polished ivory, with the pommel and hand guard made of dark cherry wood with brass accents.

"I leave it in its scabbard," Cursor said, eyes still fixed on the weapon. "I promised myself after Braduhenna not to draw it in anger ever again."

Adela placed her hands on his shoulders, causing him to shudder. It was a strange reaction, given how much he always cherished even her slightest touch. He let out a sigh and shook his head.

"I refused to marry you until you left that life behind," Adela observed. "But it never really left you did it?"

"Believe me, my love," he said reaching one hand back and clasping hers, "I never wanted to subject you to the life of a soldier's wife. When I sheathed my sword for the last time, I thought that time was over for me. We would return to Rome and start our lives anew, and I'd find a posting more fitting an Equite, where I could best serve the Empire."

"But you've done that," Adela insisted as she stepped around and sat on his lap. His face bore an expression of deep vexation, and so she put her arms around him and rested her head on top of his. "You've been appointed a Quaestor. That is an honorable position, and you've told me that you enjoy your work."

"I do," Cursor nodded, relishing the feel and smell of his wife as he turned his head to the side and closed his eyes. "Whatever Tiberius' faults, and he has many, he keeps a tight fist on the Empire's fortunes. Whether the masses know it or not, Rome's coffers swell, and we are economically stronger now than at any time in history. I am pleased to be a part of that. But for all that prosperity, there is a blackness that grows within the heart of the Empire. I see innocent men, and even women, brought down on unjust charges of treason, all to placate one man's unbridled ambition."

"I heard you fell afoul of one of Sejanus' supporters in the Senate," Adela remarked. "Calvinus' wife, Petronia, told me. Is that what keeps you from our bed?"

With his left arm still clutched around Adela's waist, he held up his spatha by the scabbard with his other hand. "When I wielded this, at least there was honesty. For all the untold pain and destruction this weapon has wrought, at least my enemies had the courage to face us like men. And above all, I *believed* back then what I was fighting for. What do I believe in now? What do I fight for?" He then threw the weapon onto the table, where it clattered across and landed on the floor. He then placed both arms around his wife's waist and held her close. She was his bastion of love and sanity in an otherwise completely mad world.

Though deeply conflicted by her husband's inability to completely let go of his violent past, Adela still loved him deeply. Their lengthy betrothal, while she waited until the day he'd no longer be compelled to draw his sword for Rome, had only strengthened their desire for each other. Since their return to the Eternal City, she had come to anticipate the change in his demeanor that came every August, around the time of the anniversary of the Battle of Braduhenna. It was on the night of the battle that Adela would see her husband go through the same ritual with the Grass Crown that he had their first night in Rome. The following day he was always returned to his self again, as if the sacramental had somehow renewed his spirit.

Her husband's words, questioning what he was fighting for, bore deep into her. And though Petronia had made it sound like their run-in with Senator Silvanus was but a trifle, deep down Adela knew that with all the injustice stemming from the iron fist of Sejanus, Cursor would not remain silent while innocents were persecuted. Cursor had survived many battles against Rome's enemies on the frontier, yet he could be rendered powerless if he made adversaries within the highest levels of Roman government.

Claudius felt he was running short on friends. Four learned scholars, all members of the Senate that he was close to, had been arrested and put on trial for treason. Two were subsequently acquitted, but had remained virtually in hiding ever since their ordeal. The third was exiled to Ponza, where Claudius' nephew, Nero, had been banished on the Emperor's orders and later died of starvation. The latest to fall, Asinius Gallus, should have come as no surprise to anyone. What unnerved him was that his brother-in-law, Sejanus, was becoming more brazen in his removing of his personal enemies. All could see it, and yet no one had the ability, or even the courage, to attempt to approach the Emperor about this. With Tiberius on his endless sabbatical to Capri, Rome was at the mercy of Sejanus.

# Chapter IV: A Burning Crisis

*April, 31 A.D.*

\*\*\*

*Gaius Caligula*

Contrary to public opinion, Tiberius was becoming concerned about the frequency of treason trials in Rome. Men, who he'd at one time considered to be close friends, and whose candor he had even encouraged, were now being brought to trial on charges of sedition and treachery.

"You give Sejanus too much power, dear uncle," Gaius Caligula said, reading the latest charge sheets over Tiberius' shoulder.

"You know I hate it when you do that," the Emperor scowled. "Don't you have duties you should be attending to?"

"Oh, that," the young man said offhand, lounging on a couch and eating an apple. "Yes, it was so kind of you to give me an appointment within the *cursus honorum*, and as a Quaestor, no less! Shame about the man I had to replace, though."

"Replace?" Tiberius asked. "I was told the position was vacant."

"Oh no," Caligula said with a laugh as he sat upright. "It was held by an Equite, though I suspect he fell out of favor with Sejanus and that dear little portly Senator Silvanus."

"Who was it?"

"Oh, let's see if I can remember…Cursor, I think was his name. Came back from the frontier a couple of years ago, after leading wild horsemen against the barbarians for gods know how many years."

Tiberius slammed his stylus down, startling his great-nephew. "Damn it all!" he barked. "Aulus Cursor is a national hero; he saved the Twentieth Legion from destruction at Braduhenna."

"Yes, I did hear about that," Caligula nodded, though still unconcerned. "I hear he gets rather uncomfortable whenever someone asks him about his being awarded the Grass Crown. Well, in that case I'll be sure I don't mention it too often." He laughed at his own private joke, though the Emperor was glaring at him.

"Cursor could easy kill you," Tiberius said coldly. "And if you were to disrespect him so, I would not even raise a finger to stop him." Caligula started to laugh again, but cut himself short when he saw Tiberius was serious.

"Have I displeased you, uncle?"

"When do you not, displease me?" the Emperor grumbled. "You know your father was scarcely any older than you when he served under me during the wars in Pannonia. And as the only one of his sons not to betray me, I would expect to get some viable use out of you!"

Caligula continued to eat his apple, although he remained silent. Two years prior, his two older brothers had been condemned of treason, along with their mother, and sent into exile. That the eldest had recently committed suicide should have unnerved the young man, although reality was he did not care about his brothers one way or the other.

"Is that why you still keep me around, uncle?" the young man finally asked. "Some days I think the only reason I still live is because you need a son of Germanicus close to you."

"You assume too much," Tiberius retorted, even though he knew his great-nephew was at least partially correct. "I still have your father's brother." This last remark caused Caligula to burst into a fit of laughter.

"Oh my!" he said, tossing the apple core over his shoulder, which a servant quickly picked up. "Uncle Claudius is but an amusing halfwit. His only use to you was as a political pawn when you approved his marriage to Sejanus' sister!"

"You are *all* pawns to me," the Emperor said with a reproving glare. "You would do well to never forget that."

"I wouldn't dream of it, dear uncle," Caligula said, leaning forward on his couch. "But you know as well as I that it is not me, nor Uncle Claudius, that you need to worry about. And if you wish to get some usage out of me, well I can think of better ways than counting coins with a bunch of stuffy bureaucrats."

Despite it being a warm spring day, Cursor found himself in a dark mood as he left the offices of Quaestor, near the Roman Senate, which he had held until very recently. The explanation given for his dismissal had been short and rather curt. Those who had at one time had hoped to use his patronage as a decorated veteran to further themselves, had decided to find other means of personal gain, once it became clear that the Tribune's patronage was not for sale. The young man who'd been assigned to replace him provided a personal connection to the Emperor, which was far more profitable than attempting to court favor with a former soldier whose sense of duty they found nauseating.

"I heard you've been replaced," Calvinus said as he joined his friend.

"Tiberius is trying to find a use for that despicable little twit, Gaius Caligula," Cursor explained. "So what does the Senate do? They appoint him as Quaestor, thereby replacing me a year before my term was up. The ignominious insult was not lost on me for a moment."

"And let me guess, the measure was proposed by our friend, Senator Silvanus."

"Astute as always," Cursor said with mock sarcasm.

"What will you do now?" Calvinus asked. "Any chance of another posting?"

"Oh yes, they found a new use for me. I'm to be made an Aedile."

The former Master Centurion halted quickly and broke into a quick laugh that Cursor could not tell was one of amusement or contempt.

"Aedile?" he asked, perplexed. "You mean to tell me that they moved you from financial oversight to registering prostitutes?"

"That is exactly what they are doing. Aedile used to be a noble office, but over the years has denigrated into little more than verifying that women wishing to sell their bodies aren't spreading anything too disgusting. I also get the esteemed privilege of verifying the licenses of bathhouses, so that those wishing to dump their spare coins as well as their seed can wash off the contagion when they are finished."

"Well we've all used our share of brothels in our time. Still, not exactly a fitting office for one who was awarded the *Grass Crown*." Calvinus' words stopped Cursor in his tracks. Were Calvinus not a veteran of the same battle, as well as part of the very legion that presented him with the Grass Crown, Cursor would have given him a sharp rebuke. The former Master Centurion was also one of the few survivors of the disastrous encounter in Teutoburger Wald twenty-two years before, who subsequently saved the lives of several legionaries, and this gave him a lot of leeway with the Tribune.

"Apologies," Calvinus said, noting his friend's dark expression.

"Please understand," Cursor explained as the two kept walking. "It's not that I wasn't honored to be presented the Grass Crown by the Twentieth Legion. That it came from the men in the ranks by gives it much esteem. You also know that I am not one to use it for political gain, yet there are many amongst both the Equites and the Senate who think otherwise. And of course those who called me 'friend' as soon as I returned to Rome only did so because they thought they could use my standing for their own gain. You are one of the few who has been honest and forthright."

"It is the way of the world we live in," Calvinus explained. "Politicians will beat their chests and praise the legions to no end, yet they either neglect or shun those very soldiers once the fighting is over. Even a number of legates who've actually led men into battle have succumbed to such pettiness in times of peace. There is little you or I can do, except continue to serve Rome within whatever capacity we are able."

"By licensing bathhouses and registering prostitutes," Cursor grumbled.

"If you wish to accept that as your lot," Calvinus shrugged. "However, know that despite the years of peace, there are still many threats to our Empire; and I do not refer to barbarians that infest the borders of the frontier."

"Explain," Cursor said, turning to face him, his brow furrowed. Calvinus glanced over the Tribune's shoulder, his mouth twitching slightly as he saw Sejanus walking down the steps of the Senate.

"In private," he stated. "Join us for dinner this evening and we'll talk."

Despite his love for Livilla, Sejanus found she tried his patience far too often. They had been lovers for years, long before the death of her husband, who had been too busy with his own cavorting to even notice. After his death, it was Livilla who became impatient. Not content with being the secret mistress of the most powerful man in Rome, she had chastised him into asking Tiberius to give his consent to their marriage. Sejanus knew it was too soon, and he cursed himself for acting so carelessly. He had further berated Livilla soundly, and let her know that if she ever wished to marry a future Emperor again, then she would have to learn patience. It was with added relief, then, that he knew the news he bore this day would finally set her mind at ease. She was wandering through the gardens in the inner court of her great house when the Praetorian Prefect called upon her.

"You're awfully cheerful today," Livilla said as Sejanus strolled into the garden. He was still in his Guards uniform, his helmet tucked under his arm. He grinned as he took her hand and kissed it.

"Your uncle has finally relented," he said triumphantly. "With his suspicious thoughts consumed elsewhere, trying to comprehend who all is out to betray him, he paid little mind when I renewed my request for your hand in marriage."

"About time the old fool saw reason," she replied, trying to downplay her feelings of elation. "When?"

"We will have to observe all the betrothal observances, of course. And you know we must follow precedent regarding which days of the year are devoid of ill omens or other celebrations. There will be some scornful mutterings, so we must not give the opposition any cause for added rebuke by scorning tradition and the gods. Not to worry, my dear, you will be mine before the year is out."

"And what of our other plans?" Livilla's eyes grew dark. "We've come too far to back down now."

"Nor will we," Sejanus assured her. "We assumed a great risk when dealing with your husband, but fortunately he made it far easier for us."

"Drusus was drunk more than he was sober," Livilla scoffed, "At least that's what the gossips all say. It was so easy to make him sleep for eternity, with no one so much as raising any suspicious questions. The hardest part was feigning sorrow in the presence of that Judean idiot, Herod Agrippa. He blames himself for Drusus' death, and while I was wailing in his arms, I so wanted to thank him for all those years they spent capering about. As I watched his tears fall, I struggled not to burst into a fit of laughter."

"He was so distraught that he left Rome," Sejanus added with a sinister laugh. "We played with fire when I asked the Emperor to approve our marriage too soon after Drusus' death, but he still had no suspicions. Now that enough years have passed, no one of importance should cause any alarm at our union; except perhaps your mother."

"To hell with her," Livilla said. "She thinks that paranoid old man on Capri is still the same devoted friend he was when she was married to my father. Never did she suspect him in the death of my brother, Germanicus. Personally, I would not have cared one way or the other if Tiberius had played a part in his murder."

"I also remember she strongly disapproved of your other brother, Claudius, marrying my sister."

"That's because a rogue like you has no business inserting himself into the imperial family!" Antonia's voice was harsh as she slowly walked up behind Sejanus, whose expression remained unchanged as he turned to face her. Livilla simply glared at her mother.

"Lady Antonia," Sejanus said with a short bow. "Please know I meant no disrespect, to either you or your family, Marc Antony's daughter."

"Ha!" Antonia retorted. She knew that the very mention of her infamous father was nothing short of contemptuous. Her parentage had been a heavy burden most of her life, eased only by the fact that her mother, Octavia, was the sister of Augustus. Though she now walked with a cane and was showing the effects age was having

44

upon her once handsome features, she had lost none of her old resolve. "You disrespected my family when you first pretended to be friends with my naïve son, and fobbed him off on your sister! I know your game, Sejanus. You were no friend to Claudius; he was but a means for you to claim a position within the imperial house."

"That bond will soon be far stronger, mother," Livilla said sharply. "Unless you've been eavesdropping on us the entire time, then you should know that Tiberius has approved our marriage." She stepped forward and took Sejanus' hand, in an open act of defiance to her mother's disapprobation.

"You may have wormed your way into the Consul's chair," Antonia said while staring at Sejanus and ignoring Livilla, "And you may have poisoned Tiberius' mind enough to convince him to let you have my daughter. But know this; I will never acknowledge you as my son-in-law!"

"And that weighs heavy on my heart," Sejanus said earnestly, though Antonia was visibly unimpressed. "I hope one day I can earn your respect, and perhaps even the love you had for our departed friend, Drusus Caesar, and all of your children."

Though his words sounded genuine, they were a cruel mockery. It was no secret that Antonia was practically estranged from her daughter, and that she had never shown anything resembling love to her son, Claudius. She did not reply, but simply glared a moment longer, before leaving through the far side of the garden.

"I hate that woman," Livilla growled, uncaring if her mother was out of earshot or not.

"You need not concern yourself with her," Sejanus said soothingly. "She knows she is powerless to stop our marriage, especially with the Emperor giving his approval. I wonder if she suspects that in due time she will be the mother of an Empress of Rome."

"I'd rather we exile her after our rise is complete," Livilla spat. "She and my stammering brother can go live together on an island somewhere for all I care."

It was an interesting change in fortunes for Cursor, one that more superstitious types would eventually say was decreed by the gods.

One of the Plebian Tribunes had fallen violently ill and was compelled to resign from his position. With Calvinus' pressuring him, Cursor had submitted his name for consideration to fill the vacancy for the remainder of the term. What surprised him was that no other candidates had elected to run against him.

"Like I said," Calvinus remarked with a grin after the formalities of the very quick election were complete, "This position does not hold the same allure that it once did. That and I may have persuaded a few potential candidates to not seek the office this time around." He gave a knowing wink at his last remark.

"You're a shrewd man," Cursor noted. "And to think, at one time you bemoaned ever going into politics!"

"I found that politics and leading men into battle are very similar," Calvinus said. "You make alliances as needed, maneuver your forces to the most advantageous position, strike the enemy where he is most vulnerable, and if you can compel potential adversaries to not even show up to fight, so much the better. Really, there is little difference between the two, except the volume of bloodshed."

# Chapter V: Unbridled Ambition

*May, 31 A.D.*

\*\*\*

*Lucius Aelius Sejanus*

"You've established yourself well, *Consul*," Silvanus said with a chuckle. "I wonder how long till the Emperor names you as his successor?"

"I suspect it will happen soon," Sejanus replied. He then showed a rare case of impatience. "By the gods, will that old bastard ever die? Hades help us if he lives as long as his cursed mother!"

"There are still a few amongst the Senate and Equites that will require disposing of first," Silvanus continued as he showed Sejanus a long scroll.

"Yes, well we do not have to rid ourselves of all of them directly. Let a few voices of opposition remain, that way the people can be duped into thinking the old order still remains. Besides, once enough of them are dispatched, the rest will fall into line readily enough. The patricians cherish their own wealth and survival far more than they do clinging to the remnants of the past. And as Tiberius has made himself so unpopular with the masses, not a single tear will fall for him once he's finally gone."

"If I may be so bold," Silvanus continued, "Were he even half as loved as Augustus, you would never contemplate your rather ambitious endeavor."

"I will grant you that," Sejanus concurred. "Lucky for us, Tiberius is not loved by anyone. The irony is that that is the one thing he longs for. Whatever his ill feelings were towards his mother at the end of her life, there was once love. I could see the angst mixed with relief when I brought him the news. And his eternal mourning for his dead son and former wife has now taken an ugly turn. His sorrow has turned to wrath."

"Dispatching Tiberius will be like putting an old dog out of its misery. So why any further delays? Why don't we strike now?"

"Because of the very men I've led for the past seventeen years," Sejanus explained, referring to the Praetorian Guard. "A number of them, especially the younger ones, are loyal to me and would doubtless welcome the transition of power. However, the majority are still sentimentalists who view their first loyalty is to the Emperor. We have to make the appearance that the Senate and people desire a regime change, and only then can I count on the Guard as a whole. Part of the reason why I concentrated them all in one barracks was so that there would be no opportunities for different cohorts to hold separate loyalties and break away from my control. And I need to make certain that he names me as his successor, thereby avoiding another civil war. It will come, and the Julians will return to power at my side; all in due time, my friend."

The faint light of the oil lamp gave an ethereal feel to Calvinus' private study. Down the corridor, in the main dining hall, his wife was hosting a dinner party for a number of their friends. Cursor's wife was also in attendance, and Calvinus made it a point of waiting until it was late in the evening before taking his friend off to his study. Both men had also abstained from drink this particular evening.

"Are we secluded enough that you can now tell me about this threat to our Empire?" Cursor asked with a trace of sarcasm in his voice.

"Unfriendly eyes and ears are everywhere," Calvinus explained, handing the Tribune a goblet of wine. Cursor noted that there were no slaves present in the study; they truly were alone.

"Are you saying we're being watched?" he asked, perplexed. This brought a short, mirthless laugh from Calvinus.

"My dear Cursor, *everyone* is being watched these days. Today in the forum I spotted at least two men who I know to be spies of Sejanus."

"How you are certain?"

"Because I've hired them before myself," Calvinus said before taking a pull off his wine. "Oh they did not know who I was, as I used an intermediary and kept myself hidden. One was undoubtedly following me, and though I cannot say for certain, my guess is the other was specifically tailing you. And of course there were probably at least a dozen amongst the crowd who were there simply to listen for anything seditious. Believe me when I say Sejanus' paranoia knows no bounds. Those foolish enough to speak ill of him in public risk signing their own death warrants."

"The entire Senate lives in fear of him," Cursor lamented. "And with Tiberius living in seclusion on Capri, there is nothing to stop his grasp for power. But how far can he really go?"

"He compelled Tiberius to name him Consul," Calvinus observed. "Sejanus is not even a Senator and therefore his appointment is illegal. Ten years ago, this would have had the Senate up in arms."

"True. One of the reasons why we had to put down the rebellion in Gaul under Sacrovir and Florus was because the Senate refused to support the initiatives of both Augustus and Tiberius to admit Gallic nobles into the Senatorial class. Even though we quickly smashed the rebels, Roman soldiers still died, and we upset the balance of power in Gaul by wiping out almost an entire generation of sons from their nobility."

"And now?" Calvinus asked rhetorically. "Now the Senate does not dare lift so much as a finger when Tiberius decides to make an Equite, whose only posting of worth has been Prefect of the Praetorian Guard, Consul."

"All legalities aside," Cursor noted, "Sejanus also has no line experience. One does not make Consul without having commanded a legion, sometimes multiple times. Sejanus is a conniving jackal wearing a soldier's uniform."

"You say what I suspect has been on your mind for some time," Calvinus noted. "Though he has blinded the Emperor to most of what actually happens in Rome, I do not think that Tiberius is completely ignorant of his colleague's aspirations. Take, for example, his only partial consent regarding the posting of legionaries to Judea."

"Of course!" Cursor said in realization. He shook his head and then started to expound upon what Calvinus had suspected for a long time. "The Judean procurator, Pontius Pilate, is an old friend and brother-in-arms, but regrettably, he is also very close to Sejanus. Granted, I cannot fault him for this. He served as Sejanus' deputy in the Praetorians, and when one seeks to improve their political standing, you find patronage wherever you can. So Sejanus gains him his posting to Judea; the most volatile province in the entire Empire."

"With ill-disciplined auxiliaries as its only soldiers," Calvinus added. "Pilate has been asking for a legion since he assumed the governorship five years ago. Yet when Tiberius finally relented, he only authorizes a single cohort, to be commanded by Pilate's own brother-in-law."

"Artorius," Cursor said, closing his eyes for a moment.

"You know I feel a close bond to him as well," Calvinus noted, Artorius' late brother having saved his life in Teutoburger Wald. "Pilate was a great soldier, and undoubtedly the best artillery officer I ever knew."

"The precision barrage he unleashed at Angrivarii allowed us to carry the ramparts with minimal loss," Cursor noted, remembering back to the final battle of the Germanic Wars.

"Agreed," Calvinus concurred. "But that was fourteen years ago. Since then he has become little more than Sejanus' puppet. A legion under Pontius Pilate would give Sejanus a massive power base. With the nearest Senatorial governor, Lamia, confined to running Syria in absentia from Rome and a weak Chief Tribune left in command, his Twelfth Legion in Syria is rendered impotent."

"So the question then is why did Tiberius only grant Judea a single cohort of legionaries?" Cursor asked. "Does he foresee a potential threat by granting them an entire legion?"

"It is only the second time that the Emperor has denied Sejanus' wishes," Calvinus observed. "The other time was when he rejected Sejanus' request to marry Tiberius' niece, Livilla. Mind you, with his sister married to the Emperor's nephew, Claudius, he is still able to claim a link to the imperial family. Were he to marry into the family, plus have a legion at his disposal in the east, his power base would be unbreakable. Perhaps the Emperor is not as blind to Sejanus' ambitions as we have been led to believe."

"I hear Tiberius did recently approve Sejanus' request to marry Livilla."

"In which case our worst fears are coming to fruition far sooner," Calvinus lamented. A long silence followed, with both men in deep thought.

"You don't think Sejanus would seek to overthrow Tiberius by force?" Cursor finally asked.

"I cannot answer that any more than you can," Calvinus replied. "Perhaps he hopes he will not have to; that he can simply wait for the Emperor to pass on to Elysium. I am fifty-two years old, and Tiberius is old enough to be my father. Yet how long will Sejanus wait? He is but a year younger than I, and his patience is not unlimited. Despite his age, Tiberius has shown no signs of being any closer to the afterlife. But know this, whatever the Emperor's failings have been over the past few years, especially since the death of his son, if Sejanus were to achieve the unthinkable, a reign of terror far worse than anything seen in generations will be unleashed."

"I know of someone who may be able to help us," Cursor observed. "He is not the most ethical of men, but he holds powerful positions within both the Praetorians, as well as the Vigiles."

"We have other friends who you will meet in due time, but unfortunately they are not in positions of political power. I suspect we will have to make some uncomfortable alliances before this is done."

"I know we have never exactly been friends," Naevius said bluntly as a slave filled his wine goblet. Cursor and Calvinus also filled theirs before dismissing the servant.

"One forms alliances where they must," Calvinus acknowledged. Cursor remained quiet, taking a drink of wine and eyeing the acting deputy Prefect. Naevius Suetorius Macro was not one of Tribune Cursor's favorite people. He was maliciously ambitious, and that he sought to gain command of the Praetorian Guard was the worst kept secret in Rome. Rumor had it that he had even gone as far as to whore out his wife to Gaius Caligula, in hopes of gaining favor.

Cursor had hoped to ally himself with someone of far more scruples, such as Cassius Chaerea. However, it was difficult to judge where his loyalties lay, for despite his devotion to duty, he utterly hated Tiberius, as well as the entire imperial family. It was no secret that he viewed it an abomination that Rome even had an Emperor. Only Claudius did he regard in any sort of friendly way, but that was only because he was completely harmless and about the only member of that dysfunctional family who did not have his eyes set on the imperial throne. Cassius, while honorable, was not one that could be completely relied upon to throw his lot in with them. As such, Cursor knew he had to forge his alliances elsewhere.

"Tell me," he said after a long pause, "What is it you hope to gain from helping us? In addition to your posting with the Praetorians, you are also prefect of the vigiles, commanding Rome's fire brigade and urban police. What are your motives for overthrowing Sejanus, besides usurping his command?"

Naevius grimaced, though Calvinus simply smiled. Cursor was known for his abject candor, which was known to gain him friends and enemies in equal measure. Of course, they did not need Naevius as a friend, but rather as a convenient ally.

"I am among the few who has direct contact with the Emperor," Naevius replied slowly, ignoring the question. "I have also befriended Gaius Caligula, which gives me even greater access to Capri. What you need is one who has such privileges, and can also act as a direct conduit between the Emperor and Senate. My motives are not your concern, but know this; if you wish to use me to cast down Sejanus, then I *will* have his command."

Though he publicly expressed his admiration and loyalty to the Emperor, on a personal level he could care less who ruled Rome. He had no love for either Sejanus or Tiberius; the Emperor was simply a means for his personal advancement. He had kept his resentment in check regarding his posting as acting Deputy Prefect while Pontius Pilate still held the actual billet. Pilate had been governing Judea for the past five years, and yet Sejanus had allowed him to maintain his status as Deputy Prefect, perhaps under the assumption that he would return to the post after his eventual return from the east. How ironic then, that once Naevius usurped Sejanus' power, Pilate would become his nominal subordinate.

Even his wife had become a useful political pawn. Naevius had allowed, in fact encouraged, her to carry on her affair with Gaius Caligula. There were few candidates left to succeed Tiberius, and Caligula was as good of a possibility as any; certainly far more probable than his stuttering uncle, Claudius!

Naevius did understand that he would never possess the level of power that Sejanus had wielded; Tiberius would see to that. However, there would still be plenty of opportunity to enrich his coffers and deal with his numerous enemies. He would also keep the young son of Germanicus close, for if he did in fact succeed Tiberius to the imperial throne, then Naevius' fortunes would be secure.

He soon took his leave, following the reassurances of both Calvinus and Cursor that the prefecture would be his, once Sejanus fell. Cursor still had another matter to discuss with his fellow Tribune once their ambitious 'friend' left.

"Tomorrow is the trial of Senator Priscus," he said, referring to the latest of Sejanus' victims brought up on charges of disloyalty.

"Yes, I know," Calvinus noted. "Another farcical show of 'justice', and yet another case of the patricians devouring each other in an attempt to show Tiberius, or at least Sejanus, who among them is most loyal."

"It is time we made a stand for justice," Cursor asserted. "I've read the indictments, as well as Priscus' supposed confession. He was at a dinner party and said a few things offhand that were foolish, but hardly treasonous."

"Priscus is a drunk, which has proven to be his downfall. Give him a chalice of wine and he won't stop talking! He is also one of the few to voice opposition to Sejanus' Consulship. But of course Sejanus will not move against him personally, as that will give the appearance of impropriety and petty retribution."

"He relies on his lackeys amongst the Julians," Cursor added. "Silvanus is his most aggressive attack dog, and he was at this party. Both the Senate and Equites are all but paralyzed now; too afraid to say anything that might offend Sejanus or the Julians, and yet ready to pounce on each other in order to remove any suspicion from them."

"We have fallen far since the days when Tiberius refused to prosecute anyone for speaking against him," Calvinus lamented. "It will undermine the very fabric of the Empire, should those who are entrusted with its rule become too enfeebled by petty squabbles amongst each other. I don't think either Sejanus or the Julians recognize the threat their grasps for power have had on the very survival of Rome herself. And even if they did, I suspect they probably wouldn't care."

"Before his arrest," Cursor said, his brow furrowed in thought, "Asinius Gallus made the mistake of pondering whether or not those opposed to Sejanus should try and gain support from the army."

"That would be a disaster waiting to happen!" Calvinus emphasized, almost choking on his wine. "Can you imagine if legionaries suddenly began thinking they could dictate policy in Rome via the sword?"

"Or worse, that they could appoint their own Emperor," Cursor added. "And if say the Twentieth Legion in Germania decided to name their Legate as Emperor, what would stop the Twelfth Legion in Syria from doing the same thing? The legions would be fighting each other instead of keeping our borders safe from invasion. It is a terrifying prospect, my friend, and one that could become a reality if we continue to allow Rome to continue in its state of dysfunction."

"The men in the ranks may be oblivious to what happens in the imperial capital," Calvinus said, "But their commanding legates are all-too-aware. If we don't secure Rome from within, in time one of them will decide to do it for us. It will be Caesar crossing the Rubicon all over again."

"Then I will make a stand for Rome tomorrow," Cursor asserted. "I know it will come with great risk, and I accept that. Since the rise of Augustus, our positions as Tribunes of the Plebs have become largely symbolic, a façade to make the people believe they still have a voice. Well, by law our responsibilities have not changed. It is time the Senate and people were reminded of this."

# Chapter VI: Hammer of Justice

*Temple of Concord, Rome*
*May, 31 A.D.*
\*\*\*

The trial had been a farce, though this came as little surprise to anyone. With the Emperor absent from the capitol, few knew his real intentions, and paranoia ran rampant. Anyone so much as accused of treason, especially by the powerful Julian clan that had allied itself firmly with Sejanus, was already damned. The Temple of Concord often served as the place where such cases were heard. With the Tullianum prison so close, and the Gemonian Stairs just beyond its steps, it was a convenient place to prosecute the damned before expediently carrying out their sentence.

Priscus sat with his council, looking thoroughly dejected. He could only hope that the magistrates who made up the court this day were feeling merciful. At best, he would be banished from Rome and stripped of all his lands and wealth. At worst…well, members of Rome's police force, the vigiles, stood ready to take the Senator away to either expel him from the city, or the short walk to his place of execution. A prominent Senator named Regulus was tasked with reading the verdict. His face was worn with strain, for he was no friend to Sejanus or the Julians. The constant affronts to justice that had permeated Sejanus' rise to power sickened him. Worse, was that he was powerless to stop it, and instead was forced to take part in the façade.

"Marcus Priscus Durio," Regulus said, reading the scroll. Priscus stood, though his head remained bowed, his face flushed and sweaty. Regulus swallowed hard before continuing. "You have been found guilty of seditious slander and high treason. You are hereby sentenced to death by strangulation, to be carried out immediately."

*"Hold!"* All was silent within the hall as Cursor quickly strode to the center of the floor. "The people still have a voice in this matter."

"What is the meaning of this?" Silvanus snapped, stepping down from his seat. "You dare interfere in the matter of this court?"

"You forget, Senator, that I am the lawfully elected representative of the people," Cursor replied calmly, holding up his Tribune's baton. "And their voice will be heard!"

Silvanus' face was contorted in rage as dozens of confused conversations started at once amongst the assembly. "By Juno, I will have you…"

"Enough!" Regulus barked. He then gazed hard at Cursor, trying to gage his intentions. It was clear the Senator was both hopeful and fearful of what the Tribune would do. "Aulus Cursor represents the people, and is sanctioned by Roman law to be their voice. Now Tribune, what say the people?"

"Senator Priscus is guilty of neither sedition nor treason," Cursor began, before he was interrupted once more by Silvanus.

"Outrageous!" the Senator complained. "He is guilty by his own admission!"

"One more word and I will have you formally censured!" Regulus said. Silvanus glared at him, but said no more. Regulus was highly respected by both the people, as well as the Emperor, and as such was one of the few who Sejanus had declared they would not dare move against. "Continue, Tribune."

"Thank you, Senator," Cursor nodded. "The only thing Senator Priscus is guilty of is being a drunken ass; hardly a crime in Roman society!"

This candid response drew some brief chuckles from the crowded hall. Silvanus' face was contorted with anger, as were those of the other Julians. Regulus allowed himself a quick smile.

"At what time were any of his words meant in a threatening or seditious nature?" the Tribune continued. "To say that the Emperor lacked the same nobility as his brother, Drusus Nero, was foolish and in poor taste, but hardly treasonous. Indeed Tiberius has even made similar assertions about himself. And to refer to Lucius Aelius Sejanus' Consular appointment as an illegal farce was also unwise, but again neither seditious nor treasonous. At no time did he ever express a desire to strike down the Emperor or Consul Sejanus. The Senator was simply voicing his opinion to those who he viewed as his friends." His gaze then fell upon Silvanus, as did a number of others. The Senator's face turned red in embarrassment, but he kept his silence.

"What then is the people's decision?" Regulus asked, gently prompting Cursor to continue. The Tribune quickly glanced at the Senators who sat on the jurors' benches. Though they had been quick to condemn Priscus, they looked relieved that any responsibility for what was about to happen now fell upon the Plebian Tribune, absolving them.

"Noble Senators and members of this court," Cursor replied. "The people have deemed the conviction and death sentence of Marcus Priscus Durio to be both improper and a travesty of justice. Therefore the proceedings of this entire trial are hereby vetoed!"

The hall immediately flew into a frenzy of a hundred different conversations and debates, with many shouting either accolades or threats towards the Plebian Tribune. Priscus stood open-mouthed in disbelief, while Senator Silvanus seethed with fury. After a few moments, the porter beat his great staff into the marble floor several times, the reverberating echo silencing the masses.

"I will not have this sacred temple defiled by such behavior!" Regulus barked. He then looked to Cursor once more, his face full of vexation. "Aulus Cursor, you have used your right as Tribune of the Plebs to veto not just the sentence, but also the conviction of Marcus Priscus Durio. Therefore, this court is now closed!" The porter next to him beat his staff into the floor once more while scribes furiously tried to write down all the proceedings.

Both jurors and observers quickly exited the hall, anxious to spread the word about the Plebian Tribune who'd overturned Senator Priscus' conviction. The vindicated man himself was ashen faced as he walked over to the Tribune, who still stood in the center of the hall, watching the crowds depart.

"I...I don't know what to say," Priscus stammered. "I thought I had no friends left in this world."

"I am not your friend, Senator," Cursor corrected, his voice firm. "You may not be a traitor, but you are a drunk and a fool. If you have any sense, you will leave Rome at once, and not come back for a very long time, if ever."

"Yes, or course," Priscus replied, giving a respectful bow. It was perhaps an odd breach of protocol, given Cursor's subordinate social standing; however, in his befuddled mind all Priscus could fathom was that he was somehow still alive. At that moment, he should have been standing at the top of the Gemonian Stairs, waiting for the noose to tighten around his neck. Instead, he would hurry home to his wife and children, and make ready to leave the city before the day was done.

One man did not share Priscus' sense of relief, and as he approached Cursor, the now-acquitted man quickly took his leave.

"You are treading in dangerous waters," Silvanus said coldly. "Be careful of the sharks you taunt."

"Are you threatening me, Senator?" Cursor replied, keeping his voice calm. Inside his heart was pounding as he tried to grasp the possible repercussions of his actions.

"Take heed, that baton which signifies your inviolability will only protect you for so long. You are simply filling in for the remainder of the term; a term which ends with the feasts of Saturnalia in December. And should you fail in your bid for reelection, what then? Perhaps you should follow your own advice and leave Rome." Before Cursor could speak, Silvanus quickly turned and followed the crowd to the large doors. His friends were consoling him while gazing hatefully towards the Plebian Tribune.

It was true that he had but seven months left in his term. And while his actions this day would undoubtedly make him well-known, he had yet to know whether his use of the Tribunician veto would gain him more friends or enemies. He surely had no reliable friends amongst the Quaestors or Aediles! And should he seek reelection at the end of the year, the Julians most certainly had ample coin in their vast coffers to fund any candidate who ran against him. He had risked much in order to save a man whom he'd never so much as laid eyes on before; a drunken fool who did not know when it was prudent to keep his mouth shut. Yet for all that, it did not matter. His position as Tribune of the Plebs made it his duty to represent the people and to enforce justice where others would not. Duty, and the love of his wife, was the only things that Aulus Nautius Cursor was certain of anymore.

He waited until most had cleared out of the temple before leaving himself. He figured he would be assailed by any number of persons wishing to hear from him what had transpired, yet he was surprised to see a number of Praetorian Guardsmen lining the top of the stairs, keeping inquisitive eyes away. He was surprised to see standing outside the temple doors was Cassius Chaerea.

"You look like you could use a friend right now," the Praetorian Tribune observed with a chuckle.

"Come to save me from Sejanus' wrath, or to escort me from Rome, as Senator Silvanus has suggested?" Cursor replied with a cocked smile. Though Cassius was more of a passing acquaintance than a friend, there was a large amount of unspoken respect between the two. Their respective military histories aside, Cursor knew that Cassius was his own man, and despite his animosity towards Tiberius, he was certainly no lapdog of Sejanus. This had doubtless led to his being passed over for certain senior billets within the Guard, which had gone to more compliant Equites like Pontius Pilate and Naevius Suetorius Macro.

"Calvinus is trying to quell the frenzy that has erupted within the Equite councils," Cassius explained. "Some are lauding you as a hero; others are calling for your removal as Plebian Tribune, or worse."

"Any word from Sejanus?"

"No," Cassius shook his head. "I did see Silvanus making his way towards his residence, though. No doubt the Julians will be furious by what you've done. However, Sejanus is clever. He will not openly rebuke your decision, especially since it saved a non-entity like Priscus. He'll have you watched and only act if you veto the conviction of one he views as a legitimate threat."

"The trial of Priscus was a drastic overreach by Silvanus," Cursor stated. "Had he gotten away with it, they would have become far more brazen. Many question who is loyal to whom. But you, Cassius, you are loyal to no man." It was a bold observation, but one that proved true by the Praetorian's response.

"I am true to my oaths," Cassius replied with an honesty that was rarely seen. "My loyalty is to neither Sejanus nor even Tiberius. My loyalty is to the people of Rome, as I suspect is yours."

"I am still loyal to the Emperor," Cursor said. "You and I have both sworn the same oaths, even if our interpretations vary slightly. Whatever his faults, it is not up to us to determine whether or not Tiberius Caesar is fit to rule Rome. If we are being honest with ourselves, the Republic is long dead, no matter what blustering old fools in the Senate may say about its possible restoration. Few of them were even alive when Augustus, subtly yet absolutely, transformed Rome from Republic to Empire. Imagine what would

59

happen if the Praetorians, or even the army, took it upon themselves to make or break the Emperor."

"It would set a dark precedent," Cassius agreed. "But right now no one is talking about making anyone Emperor. Tiberius Julius Caesar still rules Rome, albeit in absentia. My concern is that although we may finally have a Plebian Tribune who takes his responsibilities seriously, your safety cannot be guaranteed."

"As long as I hold office, my person is inviolable," Cursor remarked. "No one, not even the lowliest scum of the gutters, would dare lay a hand on me."

"Not all are superstitious of Rome's sacred laws," Cassius stated. "And if there are those willing to commit sacrilege, you can bet Silvanus will try and find them. I'm not saying you are in danger, but I would feel more comfortable if you'd allow me to detach a few of my men to see to your protection."

"I'll not live in fear like these damned paranoid Senators!" Cursor retorted. "They surround themselves with bodyguards and jump at the sound of a mouse; I will not be a part of that."

"Then you will at least forgive me if I spare the occasional patrol near your residence," Cassius replied. "Those who fall under my cohorts are good men, solid in their loyalty."

"I would expect nothing less of any who serve under you," Cursor said with a nod of respect.

"You went too far, and our 'friend', Tribune Cursor, simply called you on it," Sejanus said, unconcerned at Silvanus' ranting.

"Well be glad he wasn't Plebian Tribune when your election as Consul was decided," Silvanus retorted. "Supposing he'd used his veto then? The more we allow him to meddle in our affairs, the more troublesome he will be. I've seen his type before; old soldiers who think that because they have cut down a few unwashed barbarians, they are somehow impervious to the perils of life beyond the battlefield."

"Then it is time to show that no one is invulnerable to our will," Sejanus replied coldly. When Silvanus raised an eyebrow, he set down his stylus and folded his hands on the table. "Oh come off it, man! I know you've got contacts in the darkest corners of the city.

The only reason why neither Augustus nor Tiberius ever sent their soldiers in to wipe out these dens of pestilence and throw the bodies into the Tiber is because they occasionally prove useful when less savory methods are needed to dispose of one's enemies."

"I promise you this," Silvanus said slowly as his mind grasped what he needed to do; "The *Savior of Valeria* will trouble us no more."

# Chapter VII: Anthem of the Dark

*May, 31 A.D.*
***

Cursor was uneasy about the thinly veiled warnings from the all-too-careless Silvanus, yet he refused to live in a world of fear. He went about his daily duties, relishing in the opportunities afforded him since his election as a Tribune of the Plebs. He had been the first to exercise his power of veto in many years, and though many feared repercussions to come from either Tiberius or Sejanus, both had been strangely quiet about the affair. As there were no other treason trials slated, at least for the time being, there was a lot of talk about what the bold Tribune would do once another patrician ran afoul of Sejanus or the Julians.

Though his mind had eased greatly since his posting as a Plebian Tribune, the hauntings of his past subdued for the time being, the latest incident had vexed Cursor greatly. He knew the risks of when he exercised his veto to save Senator Priscus, and because of this he was now the subject of much unwanted attention. There were those who called upon him to act as the voice of opposition against Sejanus, and this was exactly what Cursor did not want. Ironically, the Praetorian Prefect himself had given a brief statement that helped quell the situation before it grew uncontrollable. He even went as far as to state that he appreciated the Plebian Tribune's candor and sense of justice, and that he hoped any future misunderstandings could be avoided. No doubt he did not want there to be a single voice for his opponents to rally behind, hence his attempt to downplay the incident.

As night crept across Rome late one spring night, there were hands at work that sought to put an end to such debate once and for all. Unable to sleep, Cursor lounged on a couch in his study, reviewing some documents that required his attention. These were mundane; a permit for a public building project that would extend one of the aqueducts to a residential area that was becoming overpopulated and in desperate need of fresh water before disease started running rampant. He was just glad that it was not more charge sheets for treason trials. His wife, Adela, lay on her stomach on a nearby couch, fast asleep. She had kept him company for as long as she was able to stay awake, and Cursor would soon be thankful that she had not retired to bed when he asked her to.

The sound of a muffled scream alerted him and he was quickly on his feet. He thought he heard the sound of hushed voices down the hall, and he cursed himself that he'd left his spatha beneath the stand next to his bed.

"What is it, love?" Adela said sleepily as she sat up and wiped her eyes.

"Shh," he replied quietly. "Something's not right." He quickly blew out the oil lamp and carefully opened the door to his study, Adela close behind him. Down the hall they could see their bedroom door was wide open, and the shadows of what appeared to be two men scurrying out from within.

"Damn it all," one of them said in a hushed tone. "Weren't nothing but a fucking maid servant!"

"Perhaps they're not in tonight," his companion replied.

"We've already been paid, so we'd best just kill everyone in the house and hope we get the 'inviolable' bastard," the first man said.

Though Cursor had blown out the light, he carried the lamp with him, its remaining oil scorching hot. As the two intruders were oblivious to his presence, he crept up to them, tossing the contents of the lamp right into the first man's face. He gave a horrid scream of pain, loud enough to wake all within the Seven Hills, as Cursor smashed his fist into his face, his knuckles blistering as they splattered with hot oil that scorched his screaming attacker.

As he grappled with the howling man, the second assailant panicked and started to run past them, straight into Adela. She grabbed his wrist just as he raised up his long knife to stab her. She instinctively slammed her forehead into his nose with a loud crunch, causing him to yelp in pain and drop his weapon. He stumbled onto the stairs, nose gushing blood and eyes tearing up, as he bounded down as fast as he was able. As soon as he reached the bottom, his companion was thrown over the railing by the enraged Tribune, falling headfirst onto the stone floor, his neck snapping as his skull was smashed by the impact. The body twitched involuntarily as copious amounts of blood pooled beneath.

The commotion had roused other members of the household staff, and an older maidservant ran out into street, calling to a passing patrol of Praetorians that Cassius had tasked with keeping an eye on Cursor's residence. The second would-be assassin, his eyes still clouded from the blow Adela had struck, and with blood seeping from his broken nose, ran straight into a rather large Praetorian Guardsman, who slammed him against the nearest wall, his sword drawn and raised to stab the man through the neck.

"Wait!" Cursor shouted as he raced down the stairs. "I want this bastard alive!"

"As you will, sir," the Praetorian said before slamming the pommel of his gladius into the man's head, knocking him senseless.

"Search the house," the Decanus who led the men ordered. "Make sure there are no more of them."

"Sir!" Half a dozen men, three of whom carried torches, quickly made their way through the house, rousing servants and dragging all into the main foyer. Adela made her way down the stairs as the men rushed past her, her hand over her forehead.

"Are you alright, ma'am?" the Decanus asked as Adela gingerly walked over to her husband and took his hand.

"I am, thank you," she replied. "That vile creature had a hard head!"

"Looks like his friend didn't," the Decanus said with a dark laugh as he noted the dead man who laid contorted grotesquely, his head cracked open with blood dripping and brain matter protruding from the gaping wound.

"I am indebted to Tribune Cassius for sending you," Cursor remarked.

"Well from the looks of it, sir, I would guess that your attackers needed protection more than you did!" As the Decanus gave another laugh, his men returned from searching both floors. They gathered all of the household servants in the foyer. Adela quickly noted that one was missing.

"We found her upstairs," a Praetorian said, shaking his head. An older slave woman put her hands over her mouth, eyes wide as tears started to form.

"Please, mistress," the woman pleaded to Adela, who nodded in reply.

"I'll go with you."

"Her daughter," Cursor explained as the two women went quickly up the stairs and down the hall to the master suite. Cursor knew his wife would try and console the grieving mother, who had been in their family's service most of her life.

The Praetorians seemed to ignore the cry of mourning that came from the bedroom. To most, slaves were a disposable, albeit expensive asset. Regarded as less than human, they hardly warranted any cries of sorrow when one met an untimely end. Indeed, the Praetorians scarcely even acknowledged what had happened to the poor young woman as Cursor explained what had transpired to the Decanus. The squad leader's face broke into a grin of appreciation when the Tribune told him about throwing the hot oil into the one assailant's face.

"Well played, sir," he said. "We'll take this other pile of shit to the Castra Praetoria. My guess is this was no mere robbery. We have a few highly skilled interrogators who will find out who hired them to kill you."

"Whoever it was, they certainly paid well," a Guardsman said as he held up the dead man's coin pouch. Inside were ten gold aurei coins. The semiconscious prisoner had the same number on him. As the gold aureus was the most valuable form of Roman currency, worth twenty-five denarii apiece, someone had paid a handsome sum for Cursor's demise. Indeed, the ten gold coins each man had been given would have constituted the wages of a legionary for an entire year.

"To attack one whose person is inviolable would be nothing short of sacrilege," another Guardsman thought aloud. "Someone with a lot of wealth wants you dead, sir."

"Or in the very least, scared into silence," Cursor added. He then addressed the Decanus. "I will accompany you the Castra."

"I'll send word to the vigiles," the Decanus added. "They will want to conduct their own investigation, plus they can dispose of that body. I don't think there will be any other would be assassins this night, or possibly any other. All the same, I will leave a couple of my men here to keep a watch on your wife and household."

"I'll not stay here without my husband after what we've been through," Adela emphasized. "I too will come with you to the Castra."

"Very good, ma'am," the Decanus acknowledged. "I'll still leave a couple men here. No doubt all of Rome will have heard of this by morning, and they can keep prying eyes away from your house."

The slave had been promised much if he were successful in finding those who would dispose of the hated Plebian Tribune. His master had given him thirty gold coins with which to pay the assassins, though the slave thought himself clever that he'd found two men who'd been eager to perform the deed for only twenty. The ten aurei he'd kept for himself would go a long ways towards purchasing his freedom.

As he approached the outer gate to the great mansion, he was quickly grabbed from behind by a pair of men in hooded cloaks. He made to scream, but caught the cry in his throat as he felt the point of a gladius against the small of his back.

"Please, don't kill me!" he said in a terrified whisper. His smugness had given way to terror, and he was certain he'd wet himself. "I…I have money, lots of it!"

"Yes, we know," one of the men said in a voice dark and sinister. "But we don't want your money, we want you."

"Me?" the slave tried to say with a nervous chuckle, "But I am nobody."

"We know that too," the other man murmured. "Now move!"

From the quick glances he'd been able to make of the men, the slave knew these were no mere robbers or bandits. Their cloaks were fairly new, as were their tunics. From what he could see, their hair was mostly gray, yet cropped neat and short. Both men were also clean shaven and did not stink like the usual brigand. Plus they said they did not even want his money; were they thieves, they would have beaten or stabbed him, taken his coin, and run off. Instead, they threw a bag over his head and led him to a waiting cart. As he started to whimper, he felt the point of the gladius pressed into his groin.

"One more sound, and I'll make you a eunuch," one of the men whispered maliciously.

The slave could not begin to sense where they were taking him, and his heart raced in fear as he wondered if something had gone wrong with the assassination. But then, the assailants did not even know who he was or who he belonged to, so how could anyone have been sent after him?

As the cart made its way along the streets, which were alive with the nighttime wheeled traffic of a city that never slept, the slave realized that in his fear he'd also defecated himself. Upon smelling the vile stench, one of his kidnappers turned around on the bench seat and kicked him hard in the ribs, uttering a few hushed words of profanity. After what felt like many hours the cart stopped. The slave could sense the light of many lit torches, and he squirmed in discomfort of lying contorted with his hands bound behind his back, as well as the further irritation that accompanied the evacuation of his bowels. He heard voices, and could tell one of the men who captured him was speaking to someone.

"Yes, sir," he heard an unfamiliar voice say. "They're waiting for you in the principia. We'll take this shit sack to the interrogation room."

Though little more than a slave, the wretched man knew that the principia was the headquarters of either a military unit, or in the case of Rome herself, the Praetorian Guard.

# Chapter VIII: Chalice of Agony

*The Castra Praetoria, Rome*
***

Cursor and Adela had been ushered into a private room, where they were soon joined, not by Cassius Chaerea, as they expected, but by Gaius Calvinus. And far from looking like he's just been woken, he was more alert than any of them.

"I am glad to find you well," he said as he embraced the Tribune and gave a respectful bow to Adela. "My friends should be here any time now."

"Friends?" Cursor asked. In an answer to his question, the door was opened and in walked the two men who'd captured the errant slave. Their hoods were pulled back, and though their garb was plain civilian clothing, Cursor could tell immediately these were not mere private citizens.

"Fellow brothers-in-arms," Calvinus explained with a smile as he clasped each man by the hand, a few quiet words exchanged between them. Calvinus then introduced the men to Cursor and Adela. "May I present, Valerius Proculus and Tiberius Draco; both former Centurions Primus Ordo of the Twentieth Legion."

"Ave, Savior of Valeria," Draco said with a deep bow to Cursor. Though he did not recognize the men, the Tribune rightly suspected that their paths had crossed, particularly during the Sacrovir Revolt and later Frisian Rebellion.

"Draco and I were once…professional rivals, if you will," Calvinus said with a chuckle.

"Rivals perhaps," Draco acknowledged, "But still we fought on the same side."

"It is an honor to finally meet you in person," Proculus said.

"The honor is mine," Cursor said, clasping each man by the hand. "I do actually know your names, and I regret that we never met before."

"I spent six months after Braduhenna arguing passage fares across the River Styx with Charon before deciding I would stay in this world a little longer," Proculus said with dark humor. The leadership of the Valeria Legion, particularly the Centurions, was well known for their leadership by example in battle, and few escaped that harrowing clash without being killed or seriously injured.

"And having finished out their service in the legions, they both work with me once more," Calvinus continued. "They serve Rome in a far less conspicuous, yet still vitally important capacity. Officially assigned as part-time military advisors to the vigiles and Praetorian Guard, their *additional duties* have kept them far busier."

"And not to sound clichéd," Draco added, "But tonight we were given the chance to help save the one who saved us on the Rhine."

"What did you find?" Calvinus asked.

Proculus tossed him a small pouch that jingled. "Too much coin to be carried by a slave in the middle of the night," he said. "We've been keeping an eye on a certain Senator's residence for some time, and when one of our men spotted the slave leaving in the middle of the night, we were alerted and set off to ascertain his objectives."

"One of your men," Cursor repeated, then shaking his head with a smile. "Just how many of you are there?"

"Enough," Draco replied with a nonchalant shrug.

"We caught up to that worthless bastard at a gambling den, down by the docks," Proculus went on. "It was Draco who overheard the entire conversation."

"Twenty gold aurei for the head of Aulus Nautius Cursor," Draco quoted. "Of course we figured that any slave who had that kind of money on his person would undoubtedly have hoped to keep a portion of what he was given by his master for himself. Greed is such a potent weapon."

"We knew Cassius had tasked a squad of loyal Praetorians with watching your street," Proculus said. Cursor noted his emphasis on the word *loyal*. "We dared not split up in that wicked corner of the city, so we decided to pursue the slave, as he would be the proof we needed to identify the one who wants you dead. It was risky, allowing the assassins to leave on their mission, but we knew the Praetorians would be close, plus we assumed the good Tribune was capable of defending himself. I am relieved to see our assumption was correct."

"I'll give that disgusting little man his due," Draco remarked. "He slipped away before we were able to discretely leave the den.

However, as we knew where he was headed, all we had to do was make our way to his master's house and simply wait for him."

"His master," Cursor noted. "You mean Senator Silvanus."

"Yes, sir."

"He doesn't know anything about who hired him," the interrogator said the next morning as he stepped out of the dark room. Inside, the Praetorian officers could hear the whimpers of the man who'd attacked Cursor and Adela, who no doubt wished he'd shared the same fate as his dead companion.

"It's as I suspected," Cassius said, his arms folded across his chest. The Tribune had been alerted about the attack, and once he knew all was safe, he decided to deal with the situation when he came on duty in the morning, after the interrogators had worked over the prisoner. "When the underlings of society are offered a substantial sum, they scarcely question where it came from."

As word of the attempted assassination had spread throughout the city with a speed only capable of rumors and hearsay, everyone from Sejanus, the Senate, and on down through every person within the Roman government, had wanted full details spelled out for them. It was surmised that within a couple days the Emperor would receive word on Capri and want to know everything. Sejanus suspected where the attack originated from, and he was silently irritated by Silvanus' carelessness. The Senator himself had kept a nervous silence. Though relieved once he was informed that the prisoner did not know who had paid him, he still had not seen or heard from his slave. He figured either the man had run off, or else fallen victim to one of countless thieves and murders in Rome's less desirable districts.

In truth, the slave was kept in a private holding cell within the Castra, practically under Sejanus' nose! The only Praetorian who knew his identity was Cassius Chaerea, who had promised to dispose of the man properly. The surviving assailant was not important enough to warrant execution at the top of the Gemonian Stairs. Instead, he would be kept alive just long enough to be torn apart by wild beasts during the next arena games.

"A personal message from the Emperor," Cursor said a few days later as he showed the scroll to his wife. "He thanks the gods for our salvation and says he will make a sacrifice to commemorate it."

"Strange, such pleasant words from Tiberius," Adela observed as she read the scroll. "I did not know he was still capable of speaking so cordially. He implores you to continue to do your duty and says he personally feels safer, knowing you still serve Rome…I see by his hand he put extra emphasis on 'personally'."

"He wrote this message himself," Cursor added, "He did not dictate it to a freedman scribe. You can tell by the way the signature matches the rest of the writing. That tells me he did not want anyone else to see this."

"But why?" Adela asked. "It's an innocuous enough letter; one that could even be expected from the Emperor in light of what happened."

"You saw it yourself, my love. It is a very subtle additional message; by writing the letter himself, and putting just a slight emphasis on how he personally feels safer with me in this position, it tells me that he is growing mistrustful of some of those closest to him. I may be reading too much into this, but I think Tiberius knows more of what's been happening in Rome during his absence than he has let on. I have my suspicions that this entire saga runs darker than we know. Thankfully, I now have friends who can find out for certain."

Cassius' disposition of the slave had been macabre but poignant, though he'd left the actual task to Calvinus, who in turn handed the pitiful creature over to Proculus and Draco. The intent was to unnerve Senator Silvanus, whose reputation for being emotionally unstable was already well-known. The slave, who had hoped to buy his freedom after the Tribune of the Plebs was murdered, was found just outside the gate of Silvanus' mansion; his severed head sitting atop the chest. Copper coins were shoved into the eye sockets, as well as lining his mouth. A handful of coins, symbolically soaked in blood, were left clutched in his hand. When Silvanus saw the display of horror, he became deathly ill and was not seen for a number of weeks.

Though it became public knowledge that his slave was found murdered, the matter of the coins remained a mystery to most, and none made the connection between the slave and the men who attacked Tribune Cursor. Silvanus, on the other hand, understood the ominous warning all-too-well. He dared not tell Sejanus, for if the Consul discovered that someone had discovered the dark secret of his closest Julian confidant, Silvanus would likely find his services no longer needed, and quite possibly end up on the wrong end of one of the treason trials he'd so gleefully endorsed.

# Chapter IX: Poison's Lingering Taste

*Late September, 31 A.D.*
\*\*\*

The months passed and Cursor continued in his duties as Tribune of the Plebs, all the while trying to determine if his suspicions were correct regarding the Emperor's message to him, or if it was simply a matter of overthinking the entire ordeal. It was Adela who made an offhand comment regarding the death of the Emperor's son, wondering if that was somehow tied to the traitor, Sejanus. The Tribune cursed himself for not speculating the same thing, though given Drusus' propensity for indulging in drink; no one had even considered that the Praetorian Prefect had had a hand in it. Now Cursor was assailed by suspicions, and given the years that had passed since the passing of the imperial prince, he would need all the skills of his friends who now served Rome in its darkest corners.

"It'll take some doing," Proculus said after Cursor made his unusual request of him. "And there are certain places which I simply will not be able to access for information."

"Understood," Cursor replied. "As a Plebian Tribune, I have right of entry to almost everywhere within the city, even the imperial palace. However, I'll only call upon there if our suspicions lead us there."

"I have a means of working into the palace that I've needed to put to use once more," Proculus said with a grin. His face then twisted in contemplation. "I have to say, you are reading an awful lot into one simple and short letter from the Emperor that you received almost four months ago. And you even said there haven't been any more cryptic messages addressed to you from Tiberius."

"True, but then Tiberius no longer trusts those closest to him, not even Sejanus. Despite the ever present turmoil within the Senate since Sejanus' tyrannical rise, there has been nothing overt to arouse the Emperor's suspicions. Therefore it has to be something from the past."

"Or it could be Tiberius' paranoia has simply gotten worse," Proculus observed. "Did you know I served under his command in both Pannonia and on the Rhine? It saddens me to hear what a

73

decrepit, suspicious recluse he has become. Still, he is my Emperor and my loyalty to him is unchanged."

"As is mine," Cursor emphasized. "I agree my suspicions may amount to nothing; however, if I am correct, then one of the keys to unraveling this plot lies with the Emperor's dead son."

"If there was something foul regarding Drusus' death, the culprits have had eight years to cover their tracks. Still, I will see what I can find."

It was an opportunity Cursor could not allow to pass him by. Though it sounded thin, his instincts told him Proculus would get them on the path he sought. And though he was reluctant to make any sort of deal with Naevius Suetorius Macro, further loathing that Naevius was able to gain access to the Emperor through that vile urchin, Gaius Caligula, he knew that such trying times called for them to make good on their unholy alliance.

"The Emperor grows uneasy," Naevius said as he joined Cursor and Calvinus at their usual meeting place that evening. "Though I have to tell you, I can no longer be certain if this is because he perceives an actual threat, or if it is mere paranoid senility."

The Praetorian's words only emphasized Cursor's assessment. Naevius was completely oblivious to what the Tribune and his companions had progressing in their depths to uncover Sejanus' ultimate plot.

"Let Sejanus and the Senate speculate for themselves," Cursor replied. "Did you prod him at all about sending conflicting signals to Rome in order to bring out his enemies?"

"I did," Naevius said with a nod. "Though to be honest, I don't think I had to. Tiberius does well enough confusing the Senate without prodding from outsiders. He sent two dispatches with me, one of which praised his colleague, Sejanus, and his supporters for their tireless and bountiful service. The other sharply chastised him for certain abuses against now disgraced nobles that were carried out in the Emperor's name. Sejanus has ruined many families, and those fortunate enough to escape death have been impoverished and exiled."

"There was a time when the Emperor refused to try anyone for treason simply for having a loose tongue," Calvinus observed. "Yet the longer he remains on Capri, the more frivolous charges are brought against good people."

"I've only used my veto once more since the Priscus case," Cursor said. "Sejanus and his cronies have since become more thorough in how tight they make their cases. I have to admit, there was one such trial where even I was convinced the accused was guilty. I almost think that the courts gave him exile instead of death simply to not provoke me into using my Tribunician veto. As it is, I am only appointed to finish out this current term, which ends at the New Year. I suspect that Sejanus or the Julians will hope that I do not seek re-election, or at least they will find their own candidate and use their substantial funds to make certain I lose."

"And because of that, time is no longer our friend," Calvinus added. "The Senate is already but a shell of what it once was under Augustus and even a good part of Tiberius' reign. If we don't act soon, then the ruling class or Rome, what's left of it, will be completely emasculated. As it is, the masses think that Sejanus rules Rome, not Tiberius, and certainly not the Senate. Thankfully, the legions have remained quiet about the matter, though that could change if Sejanus triumphs. I cannot fathom too many legionaries, let alone their commanding legates, who would take kindly to the Emperor being usurped by one of his own Praetorians."

"It is not just that we seek to save Tiberius from being overthrown," Cursor remarked. "If we do not stop Sejanus, we run the very real risk of civil war. I have friends still in Germania who keep me abreast on all the happenings within the Rhine army. Given the concentration of their forces on the frontier, plus their relative proximity to Rome when compared to the rest of the legions dispersed throughout the Empire, there could be anywhere from ten to twenty thousand legionaries marching on Rome within a month to install one of their own legates as Caesar."

"And unfortunately, I cannot act directly for the time being," Naevius said. "Sejanus admonished me severely for not bringing the Emperor's messages to him before delivering them to the Senate. No doubt he would have burned the scroll reprimanding him for his abuses. As it stands, I am no longer permitted unescorted access to Capri."

"Well there's a setback," Calvinus grumbled. "With time running out, we are now even more isolated from the Emperor."

"Perhaps," Cursor said thoughtfully, his hands clenched in front of his face. He then turned to Naevius. "You are still willing to be the one to strike, correct?"

"Of course. You gave me your word that once Sejanus falls, the Praetorian Guard is mine."

"A price we are willing to pay for saving the Empire from destroying itself," Cursor concurred. "And I will state it exactly that way to the Emperor."

"If you can ever find a way to see him," Naevius muttered. "Good luck with that!"

"Leave that to us," Cursor replied. "And now you may go. Let us handle the details from here, and we will let you know when it is time to act. Be advised, it will come sooner rather than later."

Naevius stood quickly, gave a short nod and left abruptly.

"He seemed almost anxious to leave," Calvinus said with a grin.

"He's too unstable to rely on," Cursor replied. "If only Cassius was more certain in exactly where his loyalties lie, I'd much sooner give him the Praetorian Guard. But no matter. Besides, I've been doing my own investigation, or rather our friend, Proculus, has started it for us."

"Oh? He made no mention to me, though I have not seen much of him in the last couple weeks."

"I'm following a trail that started with a hunch after that letter I received from the Emperor. If I am correct, Tiberius' son, Drusus Caesar, did not die of natural causes."

"No, he drank himself to death," Calvinus scoffed, ironically taking a pull off his wine.

"Literally, yes," Cursor replied. "But he did not die of excessive drink or a failed liver. He was murdered."

"Can you prove it?" Calvinus' expression showed that he believed his friend's assertion to be plausible.

"I can. Just give me some time. Proculus is seeking out Livilla's physician; a man named Eudemus. No doubt he attended to Drusus during his illness."

"There is something else I have heard, that our friend Naevius is unaware of," Calvinus remarked. "It would seem that in his ongoing contradictions, Tiberius has finally relented and allowed Sejanus to be betrothed to his niece, Livilla."

"Well that we already know," Cursor remarked offhand, "As does Naevius."

"True," Calvinus accepted. "However, our friend, Draco, has learned that the Emperor intends to resign from his position as Consul. As his colleague, this will force Sejanus to do likewise, with new Consuls elected to finish out the term. Deprived of the consulship, Sejanus will no longer hold criminal immunity. If your hunch proves correct that Tiberius no longer trusts Sejanus, this may be the opportunity we need."

"We're getting close," Cursor noted. "All that remains is we get the final pieces of irrefutable proof that Sejanus seeks to make himself Caesar. I think it is time I called upon the imperial palace to pay my respects to a potential friend."

Claudius was beaming when Cursor was announced. He hurriedly stood from his desk, which was piled with books, quills, and ink fountains.

"Y…you are most welcome!" he said, taking Cursor's extended hand.

"Thank you," the Tribune replied. "I see you are hard at work, so I hope I am not interfering."

"Not at all," Claudius assured him. "It's j…just a history of the Etruscans I've been working on for some time. I f…find them to be a fascinating people, yet most tell me my works about them are rather dry and b…boring. You know I've thought about writing a history of my family, starting with my grandmother, Livia, after her marriage to Augustus."

"That would be a fascinating read!" Cursor said with genuine interest. "I would be curious to hear your thoughts about your father, the noble Drusus Nero."

"Sadly I never knew him," Claudius replied. "I was barely a year old when he departed for Elysium. I know he was very close with my uncle, but you can guess how difficult it will be getting any useful information from him."

"It seems a bit stuffy in here, and it is such a beautiful day," Cursor observed. "I have never walked through the imperial gardens and would love to see them. Of course if it is too much inconvenience…"

"Not at all," Claudius said quickly. "I j…just have to walk a bit slow is all. I curse myself for sitting all day, when I find a good stretch of the legs actually helps my limp."

The sun shone brightly upon the gardens that decorated the courtyards of the imperial palace. Cursor had never even visited the palace before, and the complex was so vast that he feared he would get lost. Claudius, having been raised as part of the imperial family, knew it all intimately. The two men were both around forty, yet aside from their similarity in age, they came from completely different worlds. Claudius talked incessantly, excited as he was to have someone to converse with outside of his immediate family and the small circle of scholars he associated with. Cursor knew that he'd lost a number of friends during the purging of Sejanus, and so he hoped to gain his confidence and see what could be gleaned from life within the seat of the Roman Empire. Even if Claudius did not have any useful information for them, what he did provide was a means of reaching the Emperor on Capri.

As they walked past a sweet-smelling row of rose vines, they encountered an unwelcome sight, at least for Claudius.

"Reduced to seeking friends amongst the Equites, are you?" Livilla goaded. Claudius would have detested his older sister, were he the type that allowed himself to loathe anyone. It was nothing short of miraculous that Claudius was even able to have feelings of love, given the way his own family acted towards him. His mother treated him with feelings ranging from indifference to contempt, his uncle ignored him completely, and his sister had never had so much as a single kind word to say to him in their entire lives. Only his brother, Germanicus, had shown him any sort of familial love, and he had been dead for twelve years.

"T…Tribune Cursor," Claudius stammered, his head twitching, "M…my sister, L...Livilla."

"Cursor," Livilla said, her head cocked to one side, eyes narrowing. "I know who you are. You're that audacious Plebian Tribune who's meddling in affairs he'd do well to avoid."

"Just doing my duty, ma'am; representing the people." Cursor's voice was hard, but calm.

78

"Hmm," Livilla snorted. "You think vetoing the sentences of traitors is serving the people? You have a twisted sense of duty, but then I would question the judgment of any who befriended my idiot brother. I see now what happens when even our lesser nobles are left on the frontier amongst barbarians for far too long." It was clear she was trying to antagonize the Tribune, perhaps so that she could find some sort of misconduct that she could report to Sejanus. Cursor was not taking the bait, although Claudius was clearly exacerbated.

"P...please, sister!" he retorted. "Y...you should n...not speak so to our g...guests!" His head was twitching badly, and his stammer was far worse than Cursor had ever heard from him.

"S...s...sorry, b...brother!" Livilla mocked him before breaking into a fit of cruel laughter. "Oh what our father would have done with you! Mother once lamented that it was a pity Augustus outlawed leaving unfit babies exposed to die. I only hope the auspices were wrong when they predicted *you* will one day be Emperor. I hope I die before such a travesty befalls us!" Her biting words struck her brother hard, and he hung his head as she laughed wickedly and left them.

"I never heard such predictions before," Cursor observed.

"F...forget them!" Claudius snapped. "It was just some old fool's prediction when I was a boy."

What he did not tell the Tribune was about the secret prophesies of the divine Sybil, that Augustus had forbidden their publication and Livia had in her later years passed on to Claudius. They predicted that both he and his nephew, Gaius Caligula, would one day be Emperor. Caligula was not even born when the foretelling was made, but it had said 'a son of Germanicus'. With his eldest brother dead and the next oldest rotting in exile, it could only mean him. Strangely enough, it also stated quite clearly that nephew would precede uncle. With Livia's passing, Claudius held the only known copy of that particular work, which he hoped Caligula had never laid eyes on. Tiberius had known of its existence, but not that his nephew possessed it. He had also not seen it in many years, since its first writing in fact, and had probably forgotten about it completely.

Claudius was clearly distraught over the confrontation with his sister, that he did not notice the servant approaching them with a small silver tray bearing a pair of wine goblets. Cursor was startled, though he kept his composure, when he saw the man. He was no slave at all, but the former Centurion, Draco. There was a small folded piece of paper next to the goblet nearest Cursor, and he grabbed both as nonchalantly as he could. Claudius did not notice as he grabbed the other goblet and down the contents in one gulp, quickly replacing the cup with such force that it bounced off the tray and clattered onto the paving stones. Draco quickly knelt down to pick it up as Cursor eyed the note. It said only two words: *Forum, sunset.*

"Forgive me," Claudius said at last. "I sometimes allow my sister to get the best of me. Will you dine with me this evening? Your company is much appreciated, and I would love for you to meet my wife, Aelia."

"I would be delighted," Cursor replied, "But sadly I cannot this evening." He then caught a glance from Draco before speaking again. "I am, however, available tomorrow evening, if the invite is still open."

"Of course," Claudius replied with a relieved smile. "Unfortunately, my wife will be gone tomorrow night, off to visit family in Capua. Are you married?"

"I am."

"Then please, know that your wife is most welcome at my table as well."

The crowds were thinning around the Forum as the sun glowed red in the west, yet there were still enough people milling about that it made Cursor's meeting with Draco less conspicuous. The Tribune leaned against a column, deep in thought as the former Centurion approached him. He had ditched the slave's tunic and now wore his familiar civilian garb with dark cloak. He carried a cylinder used for storing books under his arm, which he thrust at the Tribune.

"A few things you might find of interest," he said in explanation.

"What I want to know," Cursor replied, taking the leather cylinder, "Is how did you do that; pose as a slave within the imperial palace?"

"Do you have any idea how large the household staff is there?" Draco responded with a short laugh. "By the gods, there must be hundreds of slaves there! Like most noble houses, the vast majority are women; however, as long as I keep silent and act like I'm supposed to be there, no one questions it. They assume I'm a eunuch and / or a mute. The Praetorians who are on duty this week are Cassius' men. They know who I am and they don't ask questions. I suspect there are more sets of eyes spying on the imperial palace than the rest of the Empire combined! There is one man, an actual slave, who is in the employ of Sejanus. He's never said anything to me, though he shoots me the curious glance whenever he sees me pop up. Of course since I never speak a word, he suspects the same things about me as everyone else. And you would not believe the sick shit I hear at that place! I am glad I spend so little time there."

"And speaking of sick shit, what are these?" Cursor held up the cylinder.

"To be read later," Draco answered. "I found certain interesting letters in a pile that looked like they were to be disposed of. I didn't have time to go through it all, so I grabbed the entire lot and stuffed them in the first thing I could find. A lot of what's in there is probably useless; however, what I did find will more than suit our purpose."

"I think," Cursor said, partly to himself, "That I should forego calling at the palace tomorrow, and instead ask Claudius dine at my house."

"Invite his mother too," Draco recommended.

# Chapter X: Antonia's Lament

*House of Aulus Nautius Cursor*
*14 October, 31 A.D.*
***

*Antonia*

There was only one person in the whole of the Empire who had unhindered access to the Emperor that even Sejanus dared not interfere with. That woman was Antonia, niece of the divine Augustus, widow of Tiberius' brother, Drusus Nero, and mother of the late Roman hero, Germanicus Caesar. A model of Roman stoicism and maternal virtue, she had kept a surprisingly low profile over the years, particularly after the ascension of her brother-in-law to the imperial throne.

"I thank you for your kind hospitality," Antonia said as servants refilled her wine cup. "It would seem my son made himself some decent friends, for once." It was meant as a compliment to Cursor and Adela, and yet it seemed Antonia could not help but partially rebuke her son.

"Please, ma'am, the honor is ours," Cursor replied. The other guests included Calvinus and his wife, in addition to Antonia and Claudius. It was just as well that Claudius' wife, Aelia, was unable to join them this evening. One could only speculate how she would react when shown proof that her brother was a traitor.

The evening progressed pleasantly enough, with Antonia delighting in the company of both Adela and Petronia. Claudius at one point whispered to Cursor that he could not recall the last time he saw his mother so much as smile, let alone laugh.

"Regrettably, she will lose that smile soon enough," the Tribune replied.

"What do you mean?" Claudius asked. Only Calvinus and Adela knew about the papers that Cursor had been sifting through for the past day. Draco was correct in that most of it was useless, but there were about a dozen or so parchments whose contents were downright damning to both Sejanus, as well as Livilla.

"My lady Antonia," Cursor said as he sat upright on his couch, holding a wine goblet high, "A toast, to your long life and happiness." The other guests exclaimed their approval, and even the old matron herself seemed pleased. It was after everyone drank that Cursor stood, his face becoming serious. "It is with deep regret that I must cast a blight on your happiness, and to yours, Claudius, my friend. It involves your daughter Livilla's betrothed, Lucius Aelius Sejanus."

"A blight has been cast on my happiness ever since I knew those two were having an affair," Antonia remarked, taking another pull of wine as her countenance darkened.

Cursor produced the scrolls he'd acquired from Draco. "Ma'am, these letters are written in a hand, and with a seal, that surely you will recognize."

"It is the seal of Sejanus," Antonia noted. All were quiet for the next few minutes as she began to read. "By Hades, these are outright treasonous! To think that the man who has seen so many condemned as traitors is by his own admission the worst of them all!"

"Sejanus seeks to make himself Emperor," Calvinus added calmly. He had spent part of the day with Cursor, who had shown him some of the more damning letters.

"I'll not ask how you came by these," Antonia stated, "Though it would seem that at least some of them are addressed to my daughter. Here he writes, *you were once destined to be an Empress, and an Empress you shall be once that old fool on Capri is disposed of.*"

"There is nothing in those that necessarily means Livilla was complicit to the plot," Cursor added. "She can readily say that she remained silent because she lived in fear of Sejanus, and that she kept the letters to use against him when the time was right."

"K…knowing Livilla, that is exactly what she'll say," Claudius observed as he absently ate a fig.

"Tiberius must be warned," Antonia affirmed.

She had privately lamented the abuses that began as Sejanus gained influence over the Emperor during the past few years. She could only watch with deep sadness as Tiberius' rivalry with her daughter-in-law, Agrippina, denigrated to the point that she and her two eldest sons were banished to tiny islands in the sea. The eldest, Nero, had perished on the Isle of Ponza the year before. And yet for all that, Antonia could not find it in her to blame Tiberius for their demise. Though not blind to the brutality the Emperor was capable of, she placed the blame squarely on Sejanus' wicked influence. It was only now, when the letters in Sejanus' own handwriting and bearing his seal were uncovered, that Antonia realized the full extent of his sinister ambition. She then asked that Cursor and Calvinus accompany her to Capri at once.

"We'll leave in the morning, ma'am," Calvinus replied.

"Your son has just finished a series of books on the Etruscan people," Cursor added. "I read a bit of it, and he has quite the genius as a scholar. I suggest you take his books to Tiberius, as a gift, and place these documents rolled up amongst the scrolls. You are one of the only people who Sejanus will not dare question for going to Capri. As Plebian Tribunes, it would be deemed acceptable that Calvinus and I act as your escorts, and also so we can pay the people's respects to their Emperor."

"Tomorrow, then," Antonia asserted. She continued with her dinner and conversation, as if it were but a formality that they were leaving for Capri in the morning to inform Tiberius that he'd been betrayed by his closest colleague. There was a noticeable tension amongst the guests, and Claudius especially started laying into the wine like he was dying of thirst. Antonia was calmest of them all. Perhaps she suspected why the Tribune of the Plebs had invited her to his house, or maybe she was just the ultimate stoic who was able to control her emotions. Whatever it was, Cursor was glad to have her with them, and was filled with both anxiety and a tentative sense of relief that they were finally able to act against the man who clutched Rome in his tyrannical fist.

# Chapter XI: No Turning Back

*Villa Jovis, Isle of Capri*
*16 October, 31 A.D.*
\*\*\*

*Villa Jovis*

The docks of the Capri harbor were bustling with activity, giving Antonia and her companions a surprising amount of anonymity. One of the Tribunes quickly located a pair of Praetorian Guardsmen, dispatching them at once to the Emperor's villa with orders to send a litter for his dear sister-in-law. Besides Antonia and the Tribunes, the only other person with them was her freedman, Pallas, who clutched the large cylindrical container full of scrolls and books. When the Praetorians in Rome had inquired about them, Antonia had explained that she was delivering a series of books, written by her son, Claudius, as a gift to his uncle. This would come as little surprise to anyone, and given Antonia's age, it only made sense that she would be escorted. Hence the presence of her freedman and the pair of Tribunes caused no alarm. Even if the Guardsmen did inform Sejanus of such a trivial matter as the Emperor's sister-in-law paying him a visit, it would not even cause him to raise an eyebrow over it. An hour passed before the Praetorians returned.

"Your litter, my lady," a Decanus said as he waved forward the dozen slaves that carried the covered lounge. A dozen Guardsmen lined either side. A person as important as Antonia warranted the greatest protection.

"I am obliged to you," she replied as Cursor helped her climb in.

The sun rose slowly behind them as the entourage made its way the few miles from the harbor to the Emperor's residence, the *Villa Jovis*. As the magnificent palace sat atop the large cliff that overlooked from the far side of the docks on the northeast corner of the island, it was clearly visible to all.

Though smaller than the imperial palace in Rome, the Villa Jovis lacked none of the grandeur. Massive columns lined the last few dozen meters leading up the sloping road, each topped by a statue of one of the many deities of the Roman pantheon. The white stone structure itself climbed high into the sky, lined with covered balconies that ran the length of every floor. Statues and fountains abounded, as did numerous evergreen trees and manmade ponds. Aside from the Praetorians who guarded the entrances and patrolled about, most of the people were slaves, although there were a few older gentlemen that Antonia recognized as philosophers and scholars. Rumors abounded of perverse excesses that had consumed Tiberius since his departure, involving both sexes, young and old alike. And yet the truth was far different, much to the chagrin of the lascivious Gaius Caligula when he came to stay with his great-uncle. The Emperor's flaws were many, particularly his wrath and penchant for brutality towards his enemies, though Antonia lamented that these were being compounded by blatant falsehoods.

"Wait here until I send for you," Antonia said as the Tribunes helped her from the litter.

"Yes, lady."

The ever loyal Pallas followed her up the long stairs that led to the second floor and the Emperor's private study. The Praetorian Decanus who had escorted the litter led them. He had offered his arm to Antonia, to help her up the stairs, but she refused.

"I am not so old and frail that I cannot walk up a simple flight of stairs," she chastised.

It was a breezy walkway that overlooked the sea which led to the large double doors where the Emperor conducted his business of the day. The two Guardsmen posted on either side opened the doors and the Decanus announced, *"The Noble Antonia!"*

"My dearest sister!" She had not heard Tiberius' voice in several years, and it brought a rare smile to her as it reminded her of happier times long gone, when her beloved husband was still in this world. Though his voice had not changed with the passage of time, his appearance certainly had.

At just a month shy of his seventy-third birthday, Tiberius was five years older than Antonia, and the strains of ruling the Empire had visibly taken its toll on him. The facial acne scars of his youth were now compounded by deep wrinkles. His once thick head of black hair had turned completely white and was thinning considerably. Even hidden beneath the folds of his imperial toga, it was clear that he'd lost considerable amounts of weight, and while his forearm muscles still showed some signs of their once epic strength, Tiberius Caesar was fast becoming a shell of the man he once was. Antonia secretly admitted that it was not just his body, but his spirit that was also greatly diminished.

"It is good to see such a welcome face," Tiberius said, taking her by the shoulders and kissing her gently on both cheeks. He then noted her somber demeanor. "You did not come just to spend time with your secluded brother-in-law." He turned his back to her and slowly started pacing towards the open balcony that looked out to the open sea.

"I have come to save you...and Rome," Antonia stated bluntly.

"I see. And who amongst my many enemies seeks my downfall?"

"It is not your known enemies, but your closest friend and confidant." Her words caused Tiberius some alarm and he quickly turned to face her, his hands still clasped behind his back. She continued, "Don't tell me you have not suspected for some time. Your cryptic messages to the Senate, both praising and berating the man you call the partner of your labors. They are not just the deluded ravings of an old man, are they?"

"The words of my son have long haunted me," Tiberius said. "He told me time and again that Sejanus was building a prison in Rome, and that once I was gone they would see the gates shut and the bolts locked down. I had hoped to assuage these doubts once and for all by forcing Sejanus to prove his loyalty to me beyond a shadow of all doubt. When he followed my lead and resigned his consulship, I thought that would silence my feelings of mistrust, yet your presence here tells me there is something more I have been kept unawares of."

"My dear," Antonia said as she signaled for Pallas to hand her the container of books. "There is much you have been blinded to these past years. I have not been told how these came to be found, but you will easily be able to vouch for their authenticity. Rolled up amongst these books are essentially confessions of Lucius Aelius Sejanus, and his intentions of replacing you as Emperor of Rome. As I cannot ascertain who they were written for, I do not know who else may be involved."

She opened the container and started to unroll the scrolls of books, handing the hidden parchments to the Emperor, one at a time. Within seconds of beginning to read the first, Tiberius' expression changed. The dozen or more messages, meant for unknown persons, damned the Praetorian Prefect of the highest treason. Finding traces of his old resolve, long lying dormant, he knew he had to act quickly. Though she had not said how she had discovered the plot against him, Antonia was one of the only loyal friends the Emperor had left.

"Drusus tried to warn me," Tiberius lamented once more, "And I did not listen. I thought their rivalry was one of petty jealousy, not that Sejanus would seek to overthrow us both." He was trembling in anger and Antonia took one of his hands in hers.

"I am so sorry," she said quietly.

"You are all I have left in this world," Tiberius replied. "It surprised me that you never remarried after my brother died. He kept me sane after I was forced to divorce Vipsania. My voyage into darkness has been long and slow, compounded over the years as all that I dared love was either taken from me, or else proved false."

"After his injury, and before gangrene took him," Antonia explained, "My husband asked me to make him a promise to never abandon you. He said, *Tiberius will rule the world someday. And when he does, he will need you more than ever.*"

"I'm amazed that he had such a sense of foreshadowing," Tiberius remarked. "Despite his infatuation with the Republic, he knew the Senate would never reassert control over Rome again. And yet, it wasn't until years after my brother's death that I became Augustus' successor…by default it seemed. Perhaps he knew that our mother's unbridled desire to force the role of Caesar upon me could not be contained."

Even after seventeen years on the imperial throne, Tiberius still resented that he had been last among Augustus' choices for a successor. And as he was already fifty-five years of age the day he became Caesar, not a day passed that he didn't wish that someone else had ascended to the imperial mantle. How much happier would he have been, had he refused Augustus' demand that he divorce Vipsania? He would never know, though every day he cursed himself for letting his courage fail him. A life in exile with the only woman he ever loved would have been preferable to ruling the world in seclusion. He had contemplated mutual suicide with Vipsania, rather than divorce, and yet the man, who had won numerous victories fearlessly leading Rome's armies to glory, could not find it in him to end his own life.

"I promised my dying husband that I would never abandon you," Antonia said, bringing Tiberius back to the present. "You have not always acted in a manner I felt best; but then, it was not I who assumed power and had to account for the welfare of an entire Empire."

"When you say I did not act as you felt I should," Tiberius muttered, "You refer to Agrippina. She blamed me for the death of Germanicus." Antonia's face twitched at the mention of her late son.

"She did," Antonia replied, trying to maintain her usual stoic demeanor. "I warned her not to take her anger towards you too far."

"Whatever promise you made to my brother," Tiberius replied, "I doubt that you would have remained loyal to me if you thought I had a hand in the murder of your son."

"It is true," Antonia admitted. "I repeatedly told Agrippina that I did not believe the rumors against you, just as in recent years I have paid little heed to the slander regarding your conduct on this isle." Whatever Antonia had thought of his actions, real or imagined, she still remained by his side, keeping a promise to her late husband.

"You have my gratitude," Tiberius said after a minute's silence. "But I fear it will do either of us little good. There is no way of telling who amongst the Praetorians I can now trust. For all I know, their loyalties lay with Sejanus, not me."

"I brought two men with me who may be able to help us," Antonia said.

"Not from the Senate, I hope," Tiberius remarked. He had little trust in most of the Senate; and besides, unless they stood unanimously with him publically, there was too much fear of reprisal from Sejanus.

"No," Antonia replied with a rare smile. She then signaled to Pallas, who ushered the two men in. The Emperor recognized Cursor immediately. His height, the fact that he was completely bald, with a prominent aquiline nose distinguished him from other men. Though he had not worn it for some time, he had elected to don his armor once more for this journey. It was immaculate, yet worn and battered from countless battles. It symbolically showed that he was willing to fight once more for the Empire.

"By the gods," Tiberius said, "Tribune Cursor!"

"Caesar," Cursor replied, snapping off a sharp salute and then clasping the Emperor's hand. "I brought with me a friend and colleague who can assist us with the Praetorians." Tiberius eyed the other man for a moment, his brow furrowed. He was older, at least in his late forties to early fifties, with numerous scars running over his right forearm, as well as a deep one across his left cheek.

"I feel I should know you," the Emperor said while assessing the man.

"The first time we met was more than twenty years ago, Caesar," the Tribune replied. "We spoke briefly after the group I was with cut its way out of Teutoburger Wald." At his statement the Emperor's eyes grew wide in realization.

"Of course!" Tiberius said. "Calvinus, is it?"

"Yes, Caesar. Gaius Calvinus, retired Centurion Primus Pilus of the Twentieth Legion and now serving as a Tribune of the Plebs."

"Then you are most welcome," Tiberius said, clasping his hand and placing his other hand on Calvinus' shoulder. "Whatever befalls me, know that I honor your years of service to Rome. To have not only survived Teutoburger Wald, but risen to the very pinnacle of a Roman soldier's career is commendable." He then waved both men over to couches that lined an ornate table. Slaves immediately appeared with wine and delicacies.

"Come, my friends," the Emperor said, taking a goblet of wine as he lay on his own couch. "No sense in deciding how to save the Empire on an empty stomach." His demeanor had quickly shifted from the shock of betrayal to one of fierce determination. He let the men eat and drink for a few minutes in silence. He wanted to allow the wine to loosen their lips a bit, as he needed their most candid assessments of what was happening in Rome. He knew he could depend upon Cursor to be candid, given their past interactions. Calvinus, he was not as certain about.

"Should Sejanus attempt to seize power, will he have the support of the people?" the Emperor asked at length.

"If I may speak plain, Caesar," Cursor began. Tiberius gave him an affirmative nod before he continued. "You've never been what one would call *loved* by the people. The divine Augustus had an aura about him that made the people adore him. Whatever his faults, they were easily forgiven. You, on the other hand, the people find culpability in just about everything you do and they loathe giving credit for your successes. Your victories in battle are mostly forgotten and that the imperial coffers have swelled with the economy thriving is largely ignored."

"That being said," Calvinus added, "The people may be at best indifferent towards you, but they hate Sejanus. He rules Rome with an iron fist, which brings about mixed feelings from the plebeians towards you. On the one hand, they blame you for granting him so much unchecked power, which has destroyed many innocent families in Rome. On the other, they feel he has manipulated you and that his edicts are not entirely yours. They want their Emperor back; or in the very least they want someone ruling Rome that is not Sejanus."

Tiberius paused in contemplation for a moment. Perhaps it was not as dire as he had feared. Indeed he did not know the extent to what Sejanus was terrorizing the populace of Rome, and for that he damned himself. At the same time he was grateful that his former right hand had proven to be so alienating.

"What of the Senate?" he asked at last. "Will they stand with me or with Sejanus?"

"The Senate is made up of mostly gluttonous cowards," Cursor replied with a trace of disdain in his voice. With few exceptions such as the new Consul, Regulus, his dealings with the Senate were passive-aggressive even on the best of days. There were many who decried his being awarded the *Grass Crown* at the Battle of Braduhenna, and many felt that his status as a national hero allowed him to undermine their authority. He had used his Tribunician veto to overrule the wishes of the Senate that he felt exploited the plebeians on more than one occasion, despite the various attempts at bribery and outright threats.

"However," Cursor continued, "They too live in fear of Sejanus; far more so than the plebeians or Equites. Whatever their animosity towards you, they would rather have an Emperor in self-imposed exile than a tyrant from the Praetorians running amok."

"It's true," Calvinus added. "And Sejanus being made Consul despite his status as an Equite inflamed their passions even more so."

"You need not worry about the Senate or the people," Cursor assured Tiberius. "Calvinus and I speak for the assembly. The other Tribunes will go whichever way we do. We will also play up to the people's sense of loyalty and the sanctity of your imperial person."

"Which leaves the Praetorians," Calvinus said.

"The Praetorians can stifle the Senate easily enough," Tiberius observed. "It would only be a matter of time before Sejanus unleashes the Guard on you. By the gods, why did I allow him to concentrate the Guard into one barracks in the city?"

"That actually may work to our advantage," Calvinus replied. "With all cohorts in one place we can assure rapid dissemination of information once Sejanus falls. As long as we keep all cohorts, as well as their officers, confined to the barracks, once word breaks that Sejanus has been arrested with the acclamation of the Senate and people, they will not so much as budge in his defense."

"This means we need an officer amongst the Praetorians to execute this," the Emperor remarked.

"We have a suitable candidate," Calvinus asserted. "His name is Naevius Suetorius Macro."

"I know who he is," Tiberius replied. "He's one of Sejanus' deputies, as well as prefect of the vigiles. How could he possibly be of use?"

"Naevius is only the *acting* Deputy Prefect," Cursor explained. "Pontius Pilate still holds the actual billet, even though he's been governing Judea for the last five years. This detail is not lost on Naevius, believe me!"

"Well is he a man of scruples?" the Emperor asked, causing Calvinus to choke.

"Hardly!" he said through a minor coughing fit. A servant quickly handed him a small towel which he wiped his face off with. "Naevius is a scheming fuck of a weasel as I've ever met!"

"What he lacks in ethics he makes up for in ambition," Cursor quickly added. "With neither Sejanus nor Pontius Pilate looking to give up their comfortable positions, he is stuck doing a job that he gets neither the pay nor status for. That he is a 'scheming fuck' as our friend Calvinus so eloquently stated makes him the perfect man to betray Sejanus."

"And I assume he will want command of the Guard should he aid us," Tiberius grunted.

"A fair compensation for saving your life and averting civil war," Cursor argued. "Believe me, I have no love for this man, yet there are times when one must make unsavory alliances."

There was a long period of silence and the two Tribunes grew noticeably uncomfortable as the Emperor brooded. When he finally spoke it was in a very slow and calm manner, which only added to the tension felt by Cursor and Calvinus. Both knew that when the Emperor's demeanor appeared most calm was when his wrath was reaching its peak.

"Naevius will have his command," he said slowly. "With plenty to keep him busy, I will see to that." Cursor and Calvinus shared a glance as Tiberius stared into his wine chalice. The two Tribunes then eyed Antonia, who had remained silent the entire time. Her expression too was one of concern by the Emperor's darkening countenance. She nodded subtly to them.

"If there is anything else you need us for, Caesar…" Cursor started to say as both men rose from their couches.

"I thank you for your loyalty," Tiberius interrupted, gazing at them once more. "It would have been just as easy for you to side with the usurper."

"I have never forgotten what you did for us on the Rhine," Calvinus quickly said, hoping to appeal to Tiberius' sense of nostalgia. Judging by the Emperor's cold expression he suspected it was a futile gesture.

"You will stay here as my guests for the night," Tiberius said, staring into his chalice once more. "In the morning you will have two official documents; one for Naevius Suetorius Macro, the other for the Senate. Know that I do not forget those who show loyalty, as well as those who betray me."

The icy chill in his voice caused both Tribunes to shiver slightly. Though certain they were doing what was right, they sensed there would be a fearsome price paid by many as a result.

"And what of you, dear sister?" Tiberius asked Antonia.

"Forgive me, but I have a beastly headache and need to lie down for a while. I would love to dine with you this evening, though."

The Emperor simply nodded as Antonia left with the two Tribunes.

"Dear gods, Cursor, what have we done?" Calvinus asked as they left the Emperor's chamber. They had declined Tiberius' offer of an escort to show them to their quarters and instead elected to take a walk along the path that faced over the cliffs into the sea. Though it was sunny and warm, the wind gusted into their faces and in the distance the sky grew ominously black.

"Unleashed a second reign of terror, I suspect," his fellow Tribune replied. "Tiberius' rage will consume not just Sejanus, but his family, as well as any friends or associates in the Senate." He paused before surmising, "We had no choice. It's as if the fates handed us two equally vile paths, and they mock us regardless of which way we choose."

"I know," the former Master Centurion replied. "I fear that many innocents will perish in the wake of the Emperor's retribution. Let Sejanus die, but what of his children? His eldest son will surely be slain, but the two youngest are still underage and blameless of their father's crimes. Yet I fear that mercy will be the last thing Tiberius will feel for some time, if ever again."

"We can't help that," Cursor observed. "We did our duty."

"And by doing so, averting a civil war," Antonia said, walking up behind them, "Not to mention further wanton persecutions from Sejanus, you may very well have saved many lives by your actions."

"Lady," Cursor said with a short bow.

"I do not envy you for the task you'll have to perform," Antonia replied, walking alongside the men.

"Nor us you," Calvinus added.

"Whatever the Senate and people think of Tiberius, he was my husband's brother and has been a loyal friend to me and mine for many decades." Antonia's assertion caused Calvinus' face to twitch. Cursor sensed immediately what was on his mind and hoped he would not say it aloud. He was to be disappointed.

"Sejanus, by his own admission, has sought to usurp the Empire for himself," Calvinus said coldly. "For that alone he is damned. Do you not fear Tiberius' reprisals may affect your household, even though it was you who warned him?" Cursor closed his eyes but Antonia simply laughed.

"Don't be daft!" she retorted. "My son may be married to Sejanus' sister, but Tiberius would not dare strike down his own nephew, who is blameless of any crime other than being a fool and a constant embarrassment to me. If anything, it may save Aelia's life."

"I wasn't speaking of Claudius," Calvinus said, turning to face Antonia. She turned and faced him, eyes narrowing. Cursor put a hand on Calvinus' shoulder, but was immediately shrugged off.

"What are you insinuating?" Antonia asked, though she already knew the answer.

"We can't prove anything yet," Calvinus replied. "But I will tell you what we suspect. Your daughter was in bed with Sejanus well before Drusus' funeral pyre sent him to the gods. It was known even to us in the legions!"

"Lady, I must speak candidly," Cursor said calmly, putting his hand once more on Calvinus' shoulder and forcing his way between them. "We now suspect that Livilla was involved in any way with the death of her husband; that he did not die of natural causes or overconsumption of drink. And if we suspect this, you can be assured Tiberius does too."

Though they expected a biting retort from Antonia in defense of her daughter, she stood in silence.

"As it was you who discovered Sejanus' betrayal," Calvinus added, "We know you must have suspected Livilla's involvement from the very beginning. That is why we do not envy your position."

"We fear that by doing your duty you may bring added sorrow to your house," Cursor said.

"Thank you for your concern," Antonia replied with a voice as cold as ice. "I am well aware of what doing my duty may cost me. Now see to it that you do yours."

An uncomfortable night followed, though as the two Tribunes had not been invited to dine with the Emperor, they did not see him again. As they made ready to depart on the ship bound for Rome the next day, a messenger rode up and hailed Cursor. He produced a single scroll, bearing the Emperor's seal.

"A personal message from the Emperor." He handed the scroll over but then stopped Cursor from breaking the seal. "Forgive me, sir, but the Emperor was very explicit. You are to open the scroll only after Sejanus has fallen."

"Did he give a clue as to what this contains?" Cursor asked.

The messenger shook his head. "Only that they are instructions for a task that must be performed by you personally. He said to think of it as a gift."

# Chapter XII: Eyes of the Tyrant

*The Senate, Rome*
*18 October, 31 A.D.*
***

After Cursor and Calvinus returned to Rome, and while their companions Proculus and Draco continued to unearth the further depths of the imperial conspiracy, it was Naevius Suetorius Macro who was to become the public face of the Emperor's rage. Two centuries of Praetorian Guardsmen were dispatched from Capri back to Rome, under the guise that they were being rotated out and that two other companies would replace them. Tiberius had vetted these particular Guardsmen personally, ensuring that they were not affected by the contagion of Sejanus. He hoped the rest would renew their vows of loyalty once their Prefect fell.

"The Senate convenes this afternoon," a messenger said as he approached the group of men disembarking from their ship. Antonia's personal litter was waiting for her as well.

"Tell them the Emperor looks forward to meeting with them," Calvinus lied. Another cover for the Praetorians coming off the ship was that the false story that they would also be escorting Tiberius himself back to Rome.

"My lady," Cursor said, gently taking Antonia's hand as he helped her into her waiting litter.

"Doing what is right is not always easy," she replied, sensing his vexation. "And sometimes it comes at a terrible price. But we do our duty and we don't look back."

A messenger had been sent to the Senate to inform them that the Emperor was coming to address them on a very important matter. It was a lie, of course. Although Capri was only a day or two's sailing from Rome, Tiberius had no intention of ever returning to the city. However, word of his coming spread like wildfire and the forum was packed with those wishing to see their long-absent Emperor.

Praetorian Guardsmen lined the path that led to the steps of the Senate. Sejanus, having received word well in advance, stood at the entrance in his full ceremonial armor, helmet tucked under his arm. Naevius knew that he would recognize the Praetorians with him and would take that as a sign that the Emperor was in fact on his way. Both sides of the path were packed with people, and the commotion was very loud. Even Sejanus' two youngest children were there with their tutor. Rumor had it that the Emperor's business dealt with their father and they were excited to see what it might be.

Sejanus furrowed his brow when he did not see Tiberius with Naevius. He descended the steps and strolled over to his subordinate.

"Where is the Emperor?" he asked.

"Just outside the city," Naevius lied. "He sent me to deliver this message on his behalf."

"Why did he not ask for me?" the Prefect asked. "I always address the Senate for him, not you."

"Well if you did," Naevius replied, holding up a scroll with the imperial seal fixed to it, "It might look rather vainglorious, if this is what I think it is."

"Explain," Sejanus demanded, cocking an eyebrow.

Naevius gave a grin and shrugged.

"He's already made you Consul," he replied. "And he emphasized to me that this message is of the utmost importance to both you and to the Empire. Perhaps your stepping down as Consul was so he could make you *Protector of Rome*. This might be a bit presumptuous, but that can only mean his successor, does it not?"

Sejanus smiled broadly and nodded in reply.

"Well then," he said, his face beaming, "You'd best deliver it."

Naevius nodded and ascended the steps. Just inside the entrance to the Senate was one of the official scribes. Naevius handed him the scroll, which the man then took to Senator Regulus, who had been appointed Consul for the remainder of the term and would address the assembly. Sejanus followed the scribe, but Naevius immediately stepped back outside. He then produced a second scroll, which he handed to the Centurion in charge of the Praetorians that were guarding the Senate house.

"You recognize this seal?" Naevius asked sternly.

"Of course," the Centurion replied. "It's the Emperor's personal mark."

"Read it," Naevius ordered. It was a very short note.

"Yes, sir," the Centurion said with a nod. That the Emperor himself would sign his name to a simple order that directed his men to stand down and return to barracks while awaiting further instructions was a bit puzzling. Still, he was a man who followed his orders, and he stepped down to the foot of the stairs.

*"Centuries!"* he shouted. *"Ready...face!"* The one hundred and sixty Praetorians who lined the steps leading into the Senate turned and faced the officer. *"Forward...march!"* He then marched his men off as the two centuries that had come with Naevius not only lined the steps, but proceeded to surround the Senate building, blocking all entrances. Their orders were not to prevent anyone from leaving, but simply to make note of those who would expedite their departure once the Emperor's message to the Senate was read. The growing crowd looked on in puzzlement. It seemed odd that the Praetorians were rotated out just as the meeting within the Senate was about to commence. Naevius then signaled for two squads of Guardsmen to follow him inside.

*"To the Noble Senate of Rome from Tiberius Julius Caesar, greetings,"* Regulus read aloud. Sejanus stood behind the platform, rather than in the Consul's chair that he'd been recently compelled to vacate. His face bore a grin of satisfaction that grated on many within the Senate who had lived in fear of him for years. The importance of the Emperor's message was lost on none of them, and there was much fear that Tiberius was in fact naming Lucius Aelius Sejanus as his imperial successor. Those Senators who were friends and beneficiaries of the Praetorian Prefect's patronage looked on with grins of satisfaction that matched his.

The Consul continued, *"Over the last few years, I have entrusted much of the administration of our glorious Empire in one man who has been the partner of my labors. That man is Lucius Aelius Sejanus. Though an Equite and not eligible for membership within the Senate, the highest honors have been bestowed upon him. I know many expressed reluctance when I did the unprecedented and elevated him directly to the Consulship. Know that your Emperor is grateful that you acceded to this request, for now I must ask your support on an issue of even greater importance."*

Regulus paused and his face twitched as he saw what the next paragraph of the scroll said. As his back was to Sejanus, the Praetorian Prefect could only assume that the pause was in deliberate suspense before he read that Sejanus was to be named Tiberius' heir. His thoughts of ultimate power came crashing down as the speaker read the rest of the scroll; his words rolling off very quickly.

*"It is with much consternation that I make this request of you. A tragedy has occurred. I, your Emperor, as well as you, the noble fathers or Rome, have been betrayed. Unable to ascertain who stands by their Emperor, or with the usurper, I am marooned outside the city, fearful of my own safety, which is why I do not deliver this message personally. The traitor I speak of is none other than the man I invested absolute trust in. Irrefutable proof has been given to me, showing that Lucius Aelius Sejanus has abused the authority of his office in order to seek to assassinate me and install himself in my place. I therefore implore the Senate to arrest Sejanus on the charge of high treason. Signed, Tiberius Julius Caesar."*

There was a shocked silence that followed, as none within the room could fully comprehend what they had just heard. Sejanus' jaw dropped, and in the confused silence, many of his followers discretely made their way to the exits, their looks of triumph turning to abject terror. None moved faster than Silvanus and the other Senators of the Julian clan. Consul Regulus quickly glanced at those who remained. Many were glaring at Sejanus with looks of utter hatred. Naevius and the squads of Praetorians quietly stepped behind their now-former Prefect.

"Noble Senators," Regulus continued, "Are we to heed the words of our Emperor and arrest Lucius Aelius Sejanus on the charge of high treason?"

*"Yes!"* one member shouted, rising and shaking his fist. The Senate chamber erupted into a frenzy as Praetorians flanked Sejanus, their weapons drawn. Before he could react, a Guardsman grabbed him from behind while another snatched his gladius from its scabbard. As the first Praetorian shoved him forward, he quickly turned and was face-to-face with Naevius.

"Why?" Sejanus asked coldly. His face was sweaty with eyes showing utter disbelief.

"You tried to make yourself Emperor," Naevius replied calmly, allowing himself a partial sneer. "And you did far worse; things that Tiberius has yet to discover for himself."

"As if you cared about Tiberius or the Empire!" Sejanus snapped, clenching his fists. Praetorians grabbed him by either arm before he could lunge at the man who betrayed him.

"Is that a confession I hear?" Naevius replied with a sarcastic grin. He then nodded over his shoulder. "Come on, at least make a good end of it."

"You're no better than me," Sejanus growled as Naevius led him out of the chamber. Members of the Senate, who had been his ardent friends and supporters, were fleeing as fast as they could, lest they too be arrested. Naevius had ordered his men outside to take note of those who fled the chamber. There would be time to deal with them soon enough.

"Your treachery will come back to haunt you," Sejanus continued as they stepped outside. The crowd was now in a state of total bewilderment as various senators fled in every direction. "I promise you share my fate one day!"

"In due time, perhaps," Naevius replied with a laugh. "But not today, and certainly not before your rotting corpse is devoured by the beasts that lurk within the Tiber."

# Chapter XIII: Punishment Divine

*The Castra Praetoria, Rome*
*18 October, 31 A.D.*

\*\*\*

*Praetorian Guardsmen*

All Tribunes and Centurions assigned to the Praetorian Guard were gathered in the Principia. Rumors had abounded regarding the arrest of their prefect, leaving many in a sense of disbelief. After leaving Sejanus in prison, under heavy guard, Cursor reluctantly accompanied Naevius to the Praetorian barracks. Calvinus had gone ahead to the Temple of Concord, where the Senate often met during times of crisis.

"You look as if this is a distasteful task for you," Naevius said as he and Cursor met in the atrium. His grin of triumph turned the Plebian Tribune's stomach. "Let us not forget, you are one of those who brought this about."

"I am aware of what I have done," Cursor replied. "Just know that you will never enjoy even a fraction of the power that Sejanus did."

"Understood," the Praetorian said with a nod. "I think you misjudge me, Tribune. Am I ambitious? Of course; but then, so was Julius Caesar. Yet I have no desire for absolute power. I see what it has done to Tiberius, and what it did to his predecessor, Augustus. No, I am quite content as commander of the Emperor's personal guard, and perhaps a governorship in the future. But understand this; your burden does not end here, and Tiberius' vengeance will not end with Sejanus." Cursor gave an affirmative nod, though his face was hard. Naevius then looked towards the door leading into the meeting chamber. "Then time to do your duty."

A servant opened the large doors and the din of commotion from the men talking frantically within immediately ceased. There were nearly a hundred officers of the Praetorian Guard clustered within. Most were in uniform, though those who supervised the night shift and had been woken with the news were in simple tunics and mostly unshaved and a bit disheveled. It was Cassius Chaerea who came forward.

"Tribune Cursor," he said with a respectful nod. "What news do you bring us?" His tone was measured and formal. As a career soldier who had dealt with far greater crises than most of his peers combined, he knew how to keep his demeanor, as well as that of his men. That Cursor was in his military Tribune's armor added to the impression that this was a far graver matter than any of them anticipated.

"Are the rumors true?" a Centurion asked. Cassius raised a hand, silencing any further questions. He then nodded to his peer.

Cursor held up a scroll that in addition to the usual wax seal was tied with a small emblem with the imperial crest attached.

"You men recognize this seal?" he stated. All nodded as he quickly broke the wax and unrolled the scroll. "*By direct order of the Emperor, Tiberius Julius Caesar Augustus, know that Naevius Suetorius Macro is hereby appointed commander and Prefect of the Praetorian Guard, effective immediately.*"

The brevity of the order only added to its immense effect. All wanted to hear about Sejanus, though it was clear what his fate would be.

"Cassius," Naevius said, "I'll not have a second-in-command who is indefinitely absent in Judea, therefore you are appointed Deputy Prefect."

"Understood."

Having no further business with the Praetorians, Cursor quickly left through the large doors. Night had fallen by the time he joined Calvinus at the Temple of Concord. They made their way through the rampaging crowds, escorted by a number of Praetorians who had come with the former Master Centurion, up the high steps leading into the temple. A Centurion of the Praetorians was waiting for them, his ear close to the massive doors.

"Well that didn't take long," the man noted with a snort.

"Is it over already?" Calvinus asked.

"Almost," the Centurion said. He then looked over to some of his men, snapped his fingers and pointed towards the Gemonian Stairs, where the most inglorious traitor in a generation was set to be cast down the steps and to the ravenous mob.

Presently, the large doors to the temple were forced open by servants, the light of oil lamps and torches within casting an eerie glow upon the steps. Members of Rome's urban police, the vigiles, lined the bottom steps, preventing the rapacious crowd from ascending the stairs. There were hundreds of people gathered, all lustily waiting for the condemned to be thrown down to them. As military weapons were prohibited within the city, most wielded clubs, though a pair of butchers carried cleavers and other vicious instruments of their trade. Torches were dispersed throughout as well, their red glow reflecting off the maddened faces of the throng.

"One can always count on the mob to be at hand," Cursor grumbled.

The crowd let out a cheer as members of the Senate made their way from the chamber and lined the top of the stairs. Consul Regulus stepped forward and raised his hands, silencing the mob. He held a piece of parchment, which Cursor guessed had been haphazardly drawn up a few minutes before, with the ink still wet. The Speaker stepped over to the Gemonian Stairs.

*"Bring forth the prisoner!"* His words caused a renewed frenzy from the multitude, which had started to grow as locals who heard the renewed commotion made their way to the forum from all directions. A squad of Praetorians drug Sejanus into the torchlight, cast by a dozen slaves who lined the small execution square at the top of the stairs. His tunic was tattered, hands bound in front with rope, and his face was beaten and swollen, with his left eye nearly

closed shut. There was no defiance left in him, only defeated resignation and sorrow. Cursor almost pitied him, but then reminded himself of what this man had done to so many innocents in his quest for ultimate power.

The Consul dramatically held up the parchment and read, *"Lucius Aelius Sejanus, you have been found guilty of high treason, conspiring to assassinate our beloved Emperor, Tiberius Julius Caesar Augustus..."* Cursor snorted at the last remark, as Tiberius was anything but loved by the Senate, or many of the people... *"You are sentenced to death by strangulation, your name to be forever damned!"*

Two Guardsmen forced Sejanus to his knees. He looked out upon the mob, then hung his head, accepting his fate. Cursor for a moment wondered if Naevius himself was going to appear and carry out the execution, but then dismissed this as preposterous grandstanding, not to mention politically foolish were he to do so. Instead, a random person, possibly a Praetorian, stepped forward, his head hidden beneath a dark cloak. He took a corded rope and wrapped it around Sejanus' neck. He then twisted the lash until it cut off all circulation and air. Cursor noticed the man leaning in close to his victim, whispering sinister things into his ear as Sejanus started to spasm with eyes growing wide. His head and body fell limp and the executioner squeezed for just a few seconds longer before releasing him. Two Guardsmen hefted the body and threw it down the stairs, where it smacked hard against the stone steps, tumbling down past the vigiles, and into the clutches of the waiting mob.

"I don't think he was dead," Cursor said quietly as the crowd started to bash the body with clubs. "He wasn't in a position to have his neck snapped, and the executioner did not hold on long enough for him to asphyxiate."

"It doesn't matter," Calvinus shrugged as the butcher with the cleaver hacked away at the condemned man's neck, severing the head to the glee of the maddened throng. "The mob finished what he started. I'm just glad this hated affair is now over."

"No," Cursor said, shaking his head as they watched the body grotesquely dismembered, the cheering masses dragging away Sejanus' mutilated corpse, to be disposed of in the River Tiber. "It is not over yet."

Tiberius' cryptic message was made plain once Cursor broke the seal on the scroll that he'd been directed to read only after Sejanus was disposed of. He then understood why Tiberius had said he should view his instructions as a gift, albeit a rather macabre one.

It was well after midnight as he made his way through the streets to the large manor house. For this tasking he wore his Tribune's armor and carried his cavalry spatha strapped to his hip. His armor gleamed in the torchlight as he, Calvinus, and squad of Praetorians approached the gate.

"I'll handle this alone," Cursor ordered as a Guardsman beat on the large door with the pommel of his gladius.

"Yes, sir," the man said, sheathing his weapon.

After a minute, the door creaked open as a bleary-eyed slave was suddenly wide awake at the sight of the armed men. In a panic, he made to slam the heavy door shut, but the Praetorians braced against it quickly, and Cursor lunged through the opening, slamming his fist in the man's nose. The cry of startled pain as the slave fell onto his backside, clutching his bleeding nose, echoed loudly through the house.

*"What is the meaning of this?"* Silvanus shouted as he descended the stairs, a servant walking behind him with an oil lamp. He stopped abruptly when he recognized Cursor's face beneath his Tribune's helm. "You? How dare you barge into my house at this hour, armed no less!"

"Senator Silvanus," Cursor said calmly, producing the scroll, "I have a warrant for your execution, signed by the Emperor. I am to present this to you, and then send you on your way into the next life."

Silvanus eyed the scroll but refused to take it. He shook his head, mouth agape, and without a word turned to flee. Cursor, being exceptionally fast on his feet, sprinted after him, tripping him before he could reach the back hall. Silvanus fell hard onto the tiled floor, the wind knocked from him.

"Come now, at least make a decent end of it," Cursor said calmly as Silvanus grunted while trying to stand once more. The Tribune kicked him hard in the stomach.

"Piss on you, Cursor!" Silvanus spat as he started coughing. "It is your corpse that should be rotting in the Tiber, not Sejanus!"

The Tribune's spatha flashed from its scabbard, his eyes now burning with anger. "This blade has not been seen since Braduhenna. I promised myself that I would never draw my weapon again in anger. You have made me break that promise! Now get on your knees and I'll at least expedite your passing."

Silvanus spit at him contemptuously and struggled to his feet once more. His anger boiling over, Cursor swung his weapon in a hard swing, the heavy and ever-sharp blade cleaving through Silvanus' upper arm. The man fell to his knees, screaming in horrifying pain as his severed limb flopped about, and blood spurting from the stump that remained. Cursor drove his spatha deep into his stomach, the weapon bursting out his back. Silvanus was no longer screaming, just gasping in horror and agony as blood and bile spewed from his mouth.

A loud screech alerted Cursor, and he saw the Senator's wife standing behind him, kneeling with her hands in her hair as she sobbed uncontrollably. As he withdrew his blade and Silvanus slumped to the floor, he had thought to simply leave his victim, knowing that it would take some time for him to die from his terrible injuries. A feeling that was best described as mercy came over him, and he knelt down to where Silvanus lay on his back, gasping for breath, eyes wide and face covered in sweat. Without another word, Cursor sliced his weapon across the man's neck, severing the artery. This elicited further screams from Silvanus' wife, though the Tribune did his best to ignore them. He threw the warrant down in front of her and promptly left, her screams echoing in his mind. The man who'd sent his assassins to kill him was dead before he even reached the door.

# Chapter XIV: Suicide's Bitter Tears

*House of Aulus Nautius Cursor*
*24 October, 31 A.D.*
***

The hour was late when a well-dressed noble woman called upon Cursor. With all focus of the past few months on the bringing down of Sejanus, those who would feel the aftereffects had almost been forgotten. It had not even been a week since the Prefect's execution, and for all anyone knew, pieces of his corpse still floated in the Tiber. And because Senator Silvanus had been executed before being granted the option of taking his own life, his estate and fortune was forfeited to the state, with his wife and children impoverished and left to seek whatever charity they could find amongst the rest of the Julian clan.

"It is late," Cursor grumbled as he sat up from his couch where he and his wife were just finishing their supper.

"Apologies, master," the servant replied with a deep bow. "She was very insistent that the matter could not wait."

"Well who is she?" Cursor asked, impatiently.

"My name is Apicata," the woman answered as she let herself into the dining hall. Cursor waved off his servant as he stood. Apicata was the former wife of Sejanus, and she was quick to explain her intrusion. Though her expression was firm, her eyes were damp and swollen. Upon hearing her name, the Tribune immediately understood the source of her bitter tears. It was no surprise that following Sejanus' execution, Tiberius ordered the death of his firstborn.

"Forgive me, but this cannot wait," Apicata insisted.

"I understand." He snapped his fingers, and another servant brought the distraught woman a large goblet of wine. As she drank, Apicata's eyes fell on Adela.

"My wife is fully aware of the circumstances," Cursor said. "I hope you don't mind her presence." When the woman did not answer, Adela stood quickly.

"It's alright, my love," she said as she kissed her husband on the cheek and promptly left the room.

"I am sorry about your son…" Cursor started to say.

"Strabo is *innocent* of his father's crimes!" Apicata snapped, her face red with anger and grief. "He is barely twenty years old, what complicity could he possibly have in Sejanus' betrayal of the Emperor?" She took a deep pull of wine and closed her eyes as she sought to regain her composure.

"Understand," she continued, trying to remain calm, "I do not fault you for bringing down that brutal tyrant. He left me for that harlot, Livilla, long before he started his usurpation of the imperial throne. I daresay she had a hand in influencing his lust for power. That woman is a demonic viper."

"So I've seen," Cursor concurred as he lay on his couch once more, Apicata occupying the one vacated by Adela. "What would you have me do?"

"I know you cannot prevent my son's fate," Apicata said, trying to keep from choking up once more. "The warrant came from Tiberius himself, rendering your Tribunician veto useless. I'm sure you've read it."

"I have. And know I would have at least vetoed the death sentence, had Tiberius not seen fit to sign the order personally. I am truly sorry."

"Thank you," Apicata continued, "But it is not your condolences that I came for. I came to give you fair warning. This hated affair is not over, even with the death of my son. As Sejanus' former wife, I cannot get a message to the Emperor, Naevius has seen to that! The only way for me to get word to Tiberius is if I name him my sole heir." This last statement caused Cursor to bolt upright as he understood the full meaning of her dark words.

"You have two other children," he said quickly. "If you take your own life, simply to get a message to Tiberius via your will, what becomes of them?"

"Their Aunt Aelia will be their guardian," Apicata explained. "As she is married to the Emperor's nephew, Claudius, they will be safer in her care than mine. Understand, I lost my husband years ago, and before this night is out, I will have lost my eldest son. I have no reason to live while waiting for Tiberius to strike down my remaining children. As long as their aunt is married to Claudius they are safe."

"But what could possibly be so important to tell the Emperor that is worth taking your own life?" Cursor pleaded.

"That will be for you to find out," Apicata said with finality as she rose. "My words to the Emperor will not be enough; he will call upon someone to ascertain the truth behind them. And given your prominent role in Sejanus' downfall, I don't hesitate to believe he will come to you for answers." She started to leave as Cursor rose from his couch and accompanied her to the door. He was beside himself that this woman, who had once been one of the most powerful in Rome, would abandon her surviving children by suicide, just to get some cryptic message to the Emperor.

"Apicata, I implore you," he said earnestly, "No child ever benefited from having their mother take her own life! If you have a vital dispatch for the Emperor, let me act as your messenger. Naevius will not stand in my way from paying my respects to the Emperor; he owes his position to me."

"Thank you," Apicata replied, her eyes looking out the open door and onto the dark street. "I will consider your offer…The sun has set, and I suspect my son has made his journey into the afterlife. I pray it was a painless passing for him."

Cursor's heart was heavy as the door closed behind Apicata. Though they'd never met before, he mourned for her. Adela quietly walked up behind him and placed a comforting hand on his shoulder.

"She won't heed your words."

"I know." If Apicata was determined to take her own life, there was little he could do to prevent it.

"Any idea what her message to the Emperor is?"

"I can only guess," Cursor replied. "And if I am correct, then it will be confirmed by Proculus' ongoing investigation."

Apicata had waited two days before deciding to follow through on her decision to end her own life. It was an unfortunate happenstance that she had seen the body of her son floating in the Tiber. Though the corpse was facedown and badly mutilated, her heart told her that is was him. Without another thought, she returned to her house, sent word for Aelia to come and take the children, then went and lay in her private bath, where she opened her wrists and watched quietly as her life flowed out her veins and mingled with the heated waters. A feeling of horror came over her at the last. As her soul departed her body, she feared that her actions would not be enough to save her children.

When word spread about Apicata's suicide, Cursor had sought out Claudius and confided in him the details of her visit to him. Fearing that Apicata's message to the Emperor might incite more reprisals against Sejanus' family and friends, Claudius had sought passage at once to Capri to see his uncle. He was less concerned about the fallen Prefect's children, Aelianus and Junilla, as they were underage and could not be viewed as a threat by Tiberius. Instead, Claudius feared for his wife, Aelia. After all, the Emperor had ordered the execution of Sejanus' eldest son, what was to prevent him from dispatching the traitor's sister as well?

Coincidentally, the only ship bound for Capri happened to carry the imperial messenger who bore Apicata's will for the Emperor. It made Claudius uncomfortable to see the satchel bearing the unknown news that for all he knew could mean the end for his wife. He silently sat across from the man in a small cabin, unable to take his eyes off the leather bag. They were the only passengers, though they said not a word to each other the entire voyage. The messenger knew who Claudius was, and while he did not know the depths of his inner turmoil, he understood enough that the entire fall of Sejanus had weighed heavily on him. He reasoned that the death of Claudius' nephew, as well as the suicide of his former sister-in-law weighed heavily on him.

Claudius did not remember falling asleep, but was glad to feel the ship had stopped at the docks, with the first rays of the rising sun making their way into the cabin.

"I'll have a litter sent for you, sir," the messenger said after they'd disembarked from the ship. As an imperial courier, there was a horse waiting for him at the docks.

"M…much obliged," Claudius replied with a tired yawn. He hated traveling by sea, and even after the short trip from Ostia, he was feeling rather ill. His limp also made the long walk to the Villa Jovis impractical. More than an hour passed, and there was little for him to do but wait. However, at length a curtained litter borne by more than a dozen slaves made its way to the docks.

Claudius climbed in and drew the curtains closed, lost deep in thought as he was carried the handful of miles from the docks to the Emperor's villa. There was little doubt that Tiberius would have read the message by the time he arrived. What had taken the litter at least an hour each way would have been covered by the courier on horse in perhaps twenty minutes.

"Why, Uncle Claudius!" The voice of Gaius Caligula startled him as he climbed out of the litter. "I didn't know you were coming to pay us a visit. Oh, what wonderful times we'll have!"

"S…sorry, nephew, but I am here to see the Emperor about a rather d…delicate matter."

"Oh, does it have anything to do with what the courier brought?" Claudius' grimace answered Caligula's question. "Well don't ask me about it, because I don't know anything. As he began to read the rather thick bundle of papers, Uncle Tiberius rather sternly told me to leave…*piss off*, is what I think he said. Still, I'm sure he'll be most glad to see you, dear uncle!"

Claudius simply shook his head and waved for the servants to open the large double doors leading into the palace. His relationship with Gaius Caligula was a rather strange one. Although the young man mocked him and played the occasional cruel prank on him, Caligula was in fact rather fond of his uncle. Perhaps it was because Claudius was the only member of their entire family that did not openly berate him as a vile monster. It certainly wasn't love, but it was the closest thing Gaius Caligula got from any of his relatives.

"By the gods, what are you doing here?" Tiberius snapped as a servant opened the door to his study and Claudius entered. "I just sent out that little reptile, Gaius, and now you let yourself in!"

"It's important, uncle," Claudius said firmly. Tiberius raised an eyebrow, surprised that his nephew was seemingly standing up to him, and without his usual stutter.

"Indeed," he replied coolly, his eyes narrowing. "Very well. I was just finishing a dispatch back to Rome." He then looked to the imperial messenger. "Dismissed."

"Sir!" the man said with a sharp salute before making for the door.

"My nephew will be returning with you, so be sure the ship does not leave without him."

"Yes, Caesar."

"Now," Tiberius said, with his hands clasped behind his back. Though Claudius could not say for certain, it seemed as if the Emperor had aged considerably since last he saw him. "What is it that my nephew feels he must travel all the way to Capri to see me about that he cannot simply send via imperial messenger?"

"If I may be b…blunt, uncle," Claudius began, quietly cursing himself for his returning stutter, "It is about my wife."

"Oh yes, that." Tiberius turned his back on him and started to pace slowly towards the open balcony where the fresh sea breeze blew in. The air was certainly cleaner than in stuffy Rome, and Claudius was just beginning to appreciate it when his uncle's words almost stopped his heart. "You'll have to divorce her."

"I…I'm sorry?" In truth, Claudius was not sure what Tiberius' disposition was towards Aelia, if anything at all. He had sought to simply reasonably ensure that she would not be harmed by his uncle's wrath. Whatever courses of action he thought Tiberius may take, this certainly was not one of them.

"Yes," the Emperor replied, turning to face him once more. "You understand I've been preoccupied with certain matters and was going to address this in due time. But since you've taken the initiative to journey here, we may as well settle this now. Your marriage to Aelia is what gave Sejanus his link to the imperial family. His betrothal to your sister may have strengthened that bond, but it was your marriage that started it all. I'll not have our family tied in any way to that of the most abhorrent traitor of our time."

"But as long as she's married to me, she is safe," Claudius noted.

"What are you talking about? She is safe, regardless. Aelia is not to blame for her brother's crimes, and she shall not be punished."

"Strabo was also innocent…" Claudius tried to catch his words in his throat, but he was too late. Tiberius' cold stare ripped into him.

"What are you saying, boy?" His voice was very calm, which Claudius knew meant his anger was rising. "You dare to question my execution of the traitor's son? And how would you know if he was involved in his father's treachery?"

"He was my n…nephew," Claudius said. He knew he'd brought out his uncle's ire, but he also knew he had to make certain assurances as to Aelia's safety, even if he would have to divorce her. "His only crime was being his father's son. There w...was no trial, just the message from you, ordering his death."

"I will *not* leave a vengeful son to seek retribution!" Tiberius snapped, slamming his fist onto a nearby table.

"Forgive me, uncle," Claudius said calmly, though his forehead was sweating profusely. He knew to leave the issue of Strabo alone, for enraging Tiberius would not help him save his wife from an uncertain fate. "Please understand my concern. I am Aelia's only protection. And as Sejanus' only sibling, his surviving children have been left in her care..."

"Yes, them," Tiberius interrupted quietly. His hands were clasped behind his back once more and his eyes darkening. Claudius did not notice; intent as he was on making good on his purpose.

"Uncle, I ask that you give me your word that no harm will come to Aelia." There was a long pause and it looked like Tiberius' mind was in another place altogether. Claudius was about to repeat himself when the Emperor suddenly spoke.

"Done!" he said. His gaze was much softer as he looked at his nephew once more. "You have my word that at no time will any harm come to Aelia. That being said, you are to divorce her immediately, and she is to have no contact with any members of the imperial family; and yes, that includes your daughter. Are we understood?"

# Chapter XV: Duty's Pain

*House of Aulus Nautius Cursor*
*November, 31 A.D.*
***

It had already been a long day for Cursor. Although not a member of the Senate, his standing as a Plebian Tribune gave him the power to veto many of their decrees. Since the execution of Sejanus, those who would seek to attain the Emperor's favor, or at least avoid the deluge of his wrath, were attempting to implicate anyone they could as a friend and accomplice of the fallen Praetorian Prefect. Cursor had taken it upon himself to intercede on behalf of those he felt wrongly accused of conspiracy.

The reality was that with Sejanus dead, all thoughts of usurping Tiberius died with him. Many of his friends had bound themselves to him simply as a means of survival. As such, Cursor had been successful in assisting many of the defendants he felt were being wrongfully prosecuted. Approximately half of those accused had been acquitted. Those convicted were given various sentences from exile to prison or death, depending upon the mood of the Senate and the courts on that particular day.

It was now six weeks since the death of Sejanus. He or Calvinus would receive an occasional cryptic note from Proculus, stating that his investigation was still ongoing and that he promised to have something substantial for them soon. Cursor was by this point exhausted by the whole affair and hoped that it would simply fade away on its own.

A loud banging on his front door would dash those hopes as servants ushered in a pair of Praetorian Guardsmen, one of whom carried a scroll in his hand. Cursor let out a sigh as the man saluted.

"Tribune Cursor?" the Praetorian asked.

"You know I am," he replied with a trace of irritation in his voice.

"Forgive me, sir. I have a message for you." Cursor took the scroll from the man and saw that it bore the Emperor's seal. As he read the contents his heart sank as he realized another wave of terror was about to be unleashed. Worse was that he was being compelled to act as the instigator of this newfound horror.

*To Tribune Aulus Nautius Cursor, greetings,*

*I have read with much interest your involvement in the trials of those accused of complicity with my former right hand, Lucius Aelius Sejanus. That so many have been acquitted shows me that, unlike the Senate, you seek justice rather than revenge or other petty motives. It also demonstrates that you have lost none of your candor as several who even I suspected of conspiring with Sejanus you were able to absolve from guilt.*

*It is due to your usual forthrightness that I feel I can trust you with what I pray will be the final chapter in this sad epic. This strikes close to my own family, and there is no one in the Senate who I can trust to find the truth. As you well know, Sejanus' former wife, Apicata, took her own life following the execution of their eldest son. Curiously enough, she willed everything to me and it was within this will that she accused my niece, Livilla, of having aided Sejanus in murdering my dear son. I have pondered these chilling words for some time and have decided that it is for you to verify these claims. If they are found to be baseless, I can rest easy, knowing it was only one who betrayed me. As much as I loathe the thought of treachery and murder stemming from within my own family, I must know the truth.*

*I rely upon you, Savior of Valeria.*

*Regards,*

*Tiberius Julius Caesar Augustus*

Cursor then remembered the conversation he and Calvinus had with Lady Antonia when they visited Capri. Whether she suspected her daughter of having murdered her husband, in the very least Antonia did not think Livilla was blameless of guilt regarding Sejanus' treason. After all, the two were betrothed and constantly in each other's company. Most certainly he had enticed her with the promise of becoming Empress of Rome. Apicata's accusation added a new level of treachery, as most, including Tiberius, had assumed for the longest time that Drusus Caesar died of overindulgence in drink. If, however, Drusus was in fact murdered by his wife, no doubt at the instigation of Sejanus, then the Emperor's fury would be renewed with even more terrifying consequences.

Cursor cringed at Tiberius referring to him as *Savior of Valeria*. It was a less-than-subtle gesture on the Emperor's part to bring up Cursor's legendary past. The Senate had disavowed the Battle of Braduhenna and only with great reluctance acknowledged the Twentieth Legion's awarding of the Grass Crown to Cursor. He had tried to suppress the memories of that harrowing ordeal. Cursor hated anyone reminding him of this, even the Emperor. However, Tiberius was correct in his assumption that such a reminder would revive the Tribune's deep sense of duty.

He hoped that Livilla, wicked woman that she was, was but another innocent victim of Sejanus' conspiring, yet his instincts told him otherwise. He knew that if it came to light that Livilla had helped Sejanus murder Drusus it would inflame Tiberius' wrath and unleash another wave of vengeance. Despite knowing this, Cursor's personal ethics would not allow him to relay any falsehoods to the Emperor, no matter how damning.

"Were there any other instructions?" Cursor asked, looking up at the Praetorian.

"Yes, sir," the man replied. "I am to escort you to the Castra Praetoria to meet with the Prefect Naevius Suetorius Macro."

"Very well," Cursor acknowledged. "If I am to go to the Praetorian barracks I'd best look the part. Wait for me here." He then started to walk towards the stairs that led to his bedroom.

A couple hours later the Plebian Tribune walked into the entrance hall of the Castra Praetoria. He had dispensed with his formal toga and was now wearing his military Tribune's armor. He spent years leading Rome's auxilia cavalry regiments on the Rhine and could not count the number of blows from enemy spears, clubs, axes, and swords that breastplate had endured. Such blemishes on his armor reminded his peers, as well as the Senate, that his career had not been spent in comfortable magistracies or bullying through unruly mobs on the streets of Rome.

His battered armor contrasted with the rest of his appearance. Cursor had made it a point to bathe and get a fresh shave before heading to the Castra. He carried his helmet under his arm and the torchlight within the hall gleamed off his bald head. As the door to the Prefect's conference room was opened he was relieved to see Gaius Calvinus waiting. Like him, Calvinus was also in full armor. Interestingly, though he had the more decorative helmet with the short horsehair crest that ran front-to-back like the other Tribunes, Calvinus was wearing his brass scale armor that he had worn as a Master Centurion, along with all of his decorations.

"Cursor, good to see you," Calvinus said, taking his hand.

"And you," Cursor replied. "I take it you received a similar letter from the Emperor?"

"It would seem so," his fellow Tribune replied. "Draco's been on a much-needed holiday ever since Sejanus' execution, though Proculus has refused to take any leave until he finds what he's been searching for. If I am correct in my assumption, what he seeks is directly related to this matter."

"I suspect Naevius is a bit irritated that it is us taking care of this little matter and not him," Cursor remarked, giving a soft chuckle as the Praetorian Prefect entered from an entranceway off to their left, accompanied by his deputy, Cassius Chaerea.

"Gentlemen," Naevius said curtly. "It troubles me that the Emperor is tasking a pair of Plebian Tribunes with a duty that he does not trust his own imperial guard to handle."

"You forget, we are not lackeys who've been sucking on the magisterial teat all these years," Cursor replied without bothering to hide his irritation.

"No disrespect intended," Naevius replied, though his voice conveyed his annoyance. He continued to walk a fine line in how he addressed Cursor. Though Prefect of the Emperor's bodyguard, it had been made plain immediately that his role was greatly diminished when compared to his predecessor. And that he owed his position to the Plebian Tribune cast an ever-present shadow. "I have not been told as to exactly what your mission requires, though I have my suspicions. I've instructed Cassius to assist you and render whatever aid you need. I expect you will keep me informed."

"You will find out when the Emperor decides to inform you," Cursor replied with a sarcastic grin. "However, if we should find what you suspect, I doubt that it will remain a secret for long." Naevius grunted and quickly left the hall.

The men tolerated Naevius and felt he was a more bearable replacement to Sejanus. However, as he had never served on the line in the legions, he did not share the unspoken bond that the three men left in the room did. In particular, Calvinus and Cassius held each other in the highest respect, having fought side by side when they extracted the band of survivors they had rallied in Teutoburger Wald. And as Cursor was the only currently living recipient of the Grass Crown, his presence alone commanded respect.

"You'll have to forgive the Prefect," Cassius said once he was certain Naevius was out of earshot. "He's a little put out at having the Praetorians used without his knowledge or consent."

"They're the Emperor's to use as he pleases," Calvinus conjectured. He then broached the subject at hand. "You know why we're here."

"Like Naevius, I can hazard a guess," Cassius replied.

"We all have our suspicions," Calvinus replied. He then took a piece of parchment off the table and scribbled some notes on it before handing it to Cassius.

"Understood," Cassius said as he read the note. "Know that whatever resources I have access to are at your disposal. I do not envy your task; it will take you to dark places."

"I fear it will take all of us to a dark place before we are done," Cursor replied glumly.

# Chapter XVI: Morally Damned

*November, 31 A.D.*

\*\*\*

*Capitoline Hill*

Cursor had made it plain that he only wanted Praetorians from Cassius' cohorts to work with him. Naevius had been puzzled by this, but said no more; glad as he was that the entire Guard was not being put at the Plebian Tribune's disposal. The one rather distasteful thing Cursor did request from Cassius was a team of reliable interrogators.

"I have a couple of men who will suit your purpose," the Deputy Prefect stated. "They're thorough, but not obsessively to the point that they get bad information or accidentally kill their quarry."

"That's good to know," Cursor replied. "Torture someone too much and they will confess to the assassination of Julius Caesar."

"Understood," Cassius chuckled. Given the unspeakable horrors the Praetorian Tribune had seen in his lifetime, inflicting pain on a suspected criminal hardly fazed him.

The men were soon joined by Proculus, who threw back the hood on his cloak and looked to be out of breath.

"By Hades, it's been a while!" Cursor said with a sense of relief at seeing his friend. "We thought perhaps you'd disappeared for good."

121

"Damn near," Proculus snorted, grabbing a cup and pitcher of water from a nearby table. "I will be so glad when Draco returns to us from his little holiday on Cyprus. I had to take his place as a 'slave' in the imperial household to find what I was looking for. He knows his way around that domicile far better than I do, and I cannot tell you how many times I ended up lost!"

"What did you find out?" Cursor asked.

"Livilla dismissed her physician, Eudemus, not long after Sejanus' downfall. Apparently she groveled profusely that she'd been manipulated and that Sejanus threatened her and her family if she so much as breathed a whisper as to his intentions. It must have worked, because although she appears to be rather skittish, there have been no signs that Tiberius would seek to have her disposed of."

"I think if the Emperor suspected Livilla as being part of Sejanus' plot, she would already be dead," Cursor surmised. "And of course she would dismiss her physician if he had knowledge that would implicate her in Drusus' murder. And that, my friend, is what we must seek out now. Sejanus has paid for his crime of attempted usurpation; now we need to uncover if the Emperor's son was also murdered."

"And how do you think Tiberius will take that?" Proculus asked, his face hard. "A number of innocents have already died in the wake of his wrath. Can you imagine what will happen if we prove that his only son was slain by his wife and her lover?"

Proculus' words sat hard with the Tribune. The sun glowed red and portentous in the west as he leaned against a pillar on the steps of the Temple of Jupiter on Capitoline Hill. The Temple of Concord, with its ominous Gemonian Stairs, was visible off to his left below. He went up there to meditate on what he needed to do. It was a pleasant enough evening, and despite it being November, the Mediterranean wind blew warm in his face. He so wanted to leave the city, but knew that he could not until his duty was complete.

"Duty," he grumbled quietly to himself. "I don't even know what that means anymore."

"It means what it always has," Adela said as she walked up behind him, "Doing what you know is right."

"Calvinus told you where to find me," Cursor noted.

"I knew you did not wish to come home and trouble me with your vexation," Adela said as she leaned against the massive pillar next to her husband. "I wish I had the answers for you, my love, but I don't."

"I feel as if I am morally damned, no matter what I do. With Sejanus dead, it is no longer solving the issue of conspiracy. Now we must find for the Emperor if his son was murdered by his own wife, and Sejanus, eight years ago."

"And do you think he was?" Adela knew the answer, but felt she needed to help her husband say it aloud.

"Without a doubt," he replied. "Apicata was so certain of it that she took her own life in order to inform Tiberius; and Livilla dismissing Eudemus tells me all I need to know. It happened the day after Sejanus' arrest, and one does not discard a physician who's been in your family for more than a decade without good reason. From what Proculus could gather, the entire household staff at the palace was at a loss as to why it happened."

"So the trick then is to find Eudemus," Adela surmised.

"No," Cursor said, shaking his head. "That will be the easy part. His only real employment has been with the imperial family, and I suspect he will try and use that as a means of gaining himself a position somewhere close. It's been eight years since Drusus' death, and I doubt Livilla told him that his dismissal was because she panicked over what would happen if he were interrogated. Proculus and Draco will find him soon enough, if they haven't already. They have eyes all over the city. It's what we do once we have him that troubles me."

"How so? If he helped murder Drusus Caesar, then he must be held to account, as well as Livilla."

"If it were only them who would pay for their crimes, then I would have no qualms about tracking him down at all." Cursor sighed deeply before continuing. "But what happens once he reveals what we already know; that he aided Sejanus and Livilla in the slow murder of Drusus Caesar? I have struggled to contain the overzealous Senate in its desire to make the ultimate example of anyone even associated with Sejanus. However, my Tribunician veto does not extend to the Emperor. How much blood will he demand in retribution for the death of his son? I'll tell you this, my love; Tiberius is not the man I once knew. His gradual decline began when Drusus died, though I cannot fault him entirely for that. And when I stood before him after Braduhenna, there was still much of the great man there."

"And now?" Adela asked, taking Cursor's hand. Though she had only met the Emperor once, she knew enough to understand her husband's terrible dilemma.

"When I saw him last, I barely recognized him. It had only been three years, yet it was like he aged more than a dozen. His voice was the only thing I still distinctly recognized. Where there was once calm, albeit cold, confidence, now I see nothing but suspicion. There was a time when Tiberius would lead men into battle, his sword among the first bloodied; utterly contemptuous as to whether he lived or died. The man who once conquered Raetia, Transalpine Gaul, and Pannonia feared nothing! When I saw him a couple months ago, it was as if he was scared of his own shadow. What's worse is his temper has become fierce, and when the Emperor flies into a rage, people can die."

"You could always allay his fears by saying that Livilla was innocent of any crime, and that Drusus did die of natural causes," Adela stated, though finding her words repugnant. "But you won't, for that would mean allowing Livilla to escape justice for slaying her husband."

"Either I allow a murderer to remain free," Cursor concluded, "Or I bring her to justice and risk inflicting the Emperor's wrath on others who were blameless."

Adela put a comforting arm around his shoulder and he looked at her for the first time. The setting sun glowed behind her, and made her seem to radiate. It was she who kept him sane in what was otherwise a dark and unforgiving world.

"Whatever Tiberius does," Adela said firmly, "Or the Senate in what they think is on his behalf, you cannot control. You shoulder much, my dear, but do not take on yourself the evils committed by others."

Cursor had steeled his resolve by the time Proculus came to see him, two days later. It was now early December, and the city was making ready for the celebration of the winter solstice later that month. Known as *Saturnalia*, it was in theory the most joyous time of the Roman year. The 17th to the 23rd was a time of gift-giving, drunken celebrations, festival parades, all accented by everyone shouting *"Io Saturnalia"*, a phrase which could mean absolutely anything. Even slaves were for a short time treated as equals, with their masters often presenting them with lavish gifts. After the strain of the past year, Cursor longed for the release that came with the celebrations that renewed one's mind and soul; and yet, when the former Centurion entered his study, he knew that Saturnalia would bring him no joy this year.

"You found him," Cursor said, noting the expression on Proculus' face.

"It took some time," Proculus replied, "But only because the city is so damned large. If he'd had the sense to leave Rome, even for someplace in Italia like Ravenna or Vesuvius, we never would have caught him. But as you suspected, he was oblivious that his dismissal was due to Livilla fearing implication in Drusus' death."

"He told you as much?" Cursor asked in mild surprise.

"Not quite," Proculus replied. "He refers to Livilla as *'that ungrateful bitch'*, and he seems to be genuinely surprised that she rid herself of his services."

"If he is truly incensed with Livilla, I suspect he would have no reservations with naming her as Drusus' killer, were it not for the fact that by doing so he damns himself."

"Which is where the interrogators come in," Proculus replied with a hard and mirthless smile.

# Chapter XVII: Imperial Fury

*Villa Jovis, Isle of Capri*
*12 December, 31 A.D.*
***

As he dismounted the horse given to him by the imperial messenger, Cursor had to repeat to himself the words of encouragement given to him by his wife. When he had delivered his candid dispatch to the Emperor following the Battle of Braduhenna, and when he brought the news of Sejanus' betrayal, there had been no joy, but at least he'd felt a sense of duty and the knowledge that he was doing what was right. This time, his feelings were mostly numb after the constant assault of contradictions. He finally had to resolve himself to the reality that doing what was right was not always easy, and in fact often came at a terrible price. Apicata's ominous words to that effect echoed in his mind.

Tiberius had been expecting Cursor for some time; ever since he sent him his directive to discover the truth about his son's death. He was in his study, exactly as the Tribune had seen him before. He was looking pale and tired, and Cursor wondered if he went out into the sun anymore. Putting on his best professional face, he stepped up to the Emperor's desk and saluted, his left hand clutching the scrolls that contained all the findings of their investigation.

Tiberius wordlessly held out his hand, and Cursor could feel the tension building as he passed the scrolls to the Emperor. He stood rigid as Tiberius read. After a long and awkward silence, the Emperor finally spoke.

"So it is true."

"Yes, Caesar." Cursor found he could not bring himself to look directly at the Emperor, and instead kept his eyes fixed straight ahead. "Eudemus confessed readily enough, and his story was verified by a slave named Lygdus, who had been Drusus' cupbearer. Eudemus had been giving Drusus a concoction to help him sleep, and it was Livilla, along with Sejanus, who compelled him to mix a dose that would *'make Drusus sleep for eternity'*."

126

To the outside observer, Tiberius' calm demeanor would have seemed out of place, given the appalling news he'd received. However, those who knew him best understood that in such situations, when his voice was most calm, his fury was reaching its peak.

"You've done well," Tiberius said, still scanning the documents in his hands. His voice was cold and devoid of any emotion. Cursor hardly even recognized it.

"If I may make a request, Caesar," the Tribune said slowly, forming his words carefully, "Eudemus and Lygdus are both in prison, awaiting execution. The only other culprit in this affair is Livilla, and I hope no others…"

"Thank you, Tribune Cursor; that will be all." Tiberius had deliberately cut him off before he could speak further, and it affirmed his fears. When he paused momentarily, the Emperor's next words bit into him. "You are dismissed!"

Wracked by renewed doubts over what he'd just done, Cursor quickly saluted and left the study. He bounded down the stairs as quickly as he could without causing a disturbance, and as he reached the large double doors, the howl of rage echoed throughout the entire villa.

*"That abominable bitch killed my son!"*

Claudius knew the message to be of the utmost seriousness, for a dispatch, even from the Emperor, did not require a dozen armed Praetorians and one of their officers to deliver it. Yet bearing the message was none other than the Prefect, Naevius Suetorius Macro. He and his men were all dressed for battle and Claudius knew that the news they brought boded ill. Naevius handed the sealed letter to Antonia, whose face was hard as stone as she read its contents.

"I understand," she said quietly. Naevius nodded.

"Yes, lady," he replied. "The Emperor has given you authority to deal with the matter as you see fit. He trusts your judgment will be both sound and *thorough*." There was an ominous tone to his voice, which combined with Antonia's cold stare caused Claudius to break into a sweat. He started to back away when he tripped and fell over a couch. While this brought a few quiet chuckles from the Praetorians, Naevius and Antonia continued to stare at each other.

"Bring her to me," Antonia said quietly. Naevius nodded and quickly turned and exited the room, his guardsmen following. It was only when the sounds of their footsteps echoing became quiet that Antonia's demeanor finally broke.

"They killed Drusus!" she sobbed.

Claudius stood dumbfounded as his mother wiped the tears from her eyes and fell to a nearby couch. He awkwardly put his arm around her. The two had never shared a close relationship and in truth Antonia was still in many ways repelled by her youngest son.

"Get off!" she snapped, shoving him away. Not knowing what else to do, Claudius picked up the letter that Antonia had dropped. He clasped his hand over his mouth as he read the contents.

*My dearest Antonia,*

*It is with sincere regret that I must confirm what I am sure you already know. No doubt you heard Apicata's accusations before her own death that implicate not only my former right hand, Sejanus, but also your own daughter, Livilla, in the death of my son. Drusus' former cupbearer, Lygdus, as well as Livilla's own physician, Eudemus, have confirmed Apicata's accounts.*

*Sejanus and his followers have paid for their crimes. The issue now arises what to do about Livilla. We can only speculate as to how my brother would have dealt with the knowledge that his own daughter was guilty of both murder and high treason. Therefore I will leave Livilla's fate to you. It may seem unfair of me to place such a heavy burden upon you, especially in light of your continued loyalty and devoted friendship. However, I also know that if given the choice, you would wish to dispose of this matter personally. Therefore, it is with a heavy heart, but also with the strongest mutual sense of duty that I leave Livilla's fate to you. Know that I do not envy you, and it saddens me that this affair has cost each of us a child.*

*Your loyalty and continued friendship are among the few things I still cherish in this world. Your devoted brother-in-law,*

*Tiberius*

Livilla's screams brought Claudius back to the present. He was numb with shock at what he had just read and could not fathom how his sister, though they had been at best indifferent towards each other all their lives, had done the unthinkable. He watched helplessly as Naevius dragged her screaming by her hair.

*"Let go of me!"* she screamed. *"I'll have your head for this, you filthy whore-fucker!"*

Claudius was not sure if he was more appalled by the Praetorian's rough handling of his sister or her undignified language. As Livilla continued to scream and claw at his burly arm, Naevius threw her forward, where she stumbled into Antonia.

"Mother…" she started to say, but was cut short as Antonia slapped her hard across the ear, sending her sprawling to the floor. Antonia then nodded to the Praetorians who in turn left the room.

*"Mother, what the fuck?"* Livilla screeched in another fit of foul language as Antonia kicked her hard in the stomach.

"Vile creature!" Antonia spat. "You murdered your own husband and sought to put a traitor on the imperial throne!" Her eyes clouded with rage and whatever love Antonia had felt for her daughter evaporated into the hatred of her betrayal. In her forty-four years Livilla had never seen such wrath emanate from her mother and she was terrified.

"No!" she shouted, quickly shaking her head. "I would never…" She was cut short once more as Antonia reached down and slapped her across the face.

"Liar!" Antonia growled. *"You are no daughter of mine!"* She reached down to grab her by the hair, but she was not quick enough and Livilla crawled over to Claudius, noticing him for the first time. She grabbed him by the toga and pulled herself to her feet.

"Claudius, please!" she pleaded. The tears that flowed down her swollen cheeks were wrought from terror rather than pain from being struck. "Dear brother, don't let them hurt me!"

Claudius' heart softened and he put an arm around his sister. The reality of the accusations against her would not sink in for the next several days and he struggled to wrap his mind around what was happening. Antonia stepped in and grabbed Livilla by the hair, dragging her away from her brother.

"Stay out of this, Claudius," Antonia said quietly. "She is no longer your sister."

The following week was heartbreaking for Claudius. Late one afternoon he limped quietly towards the room where Livilla had been imprisoned by her mother. The door was now open and inside he could see servants wrapping her emaciated body into a sheet. It had taken a full week for starvation and dehydration to claim his sister and send her to whatever fate awaited her in the next life. Antonia had sat outside the door, listening to her daughter's cries, throughout the ordeal. She ate and drank just enough to sustain herself and as Claudius gazed upon her she looked as if she had aged a dozen years. Whatever pity he had felt for his sister had slowly dissipated as he comprehended the wickedness within her soul. Drusus had been a close friend, and to know that Livilla had slowly poisoned him over a period of months so that his death would not raise suspicion filled Claudius with revulsion and sadness.

Of course he had not been completely spared either during the downfall of Sejanus. Per his uncle's directive, he divorced his wife, Aelia, as it would not do for the traitor's sister to remain a part of the imperial household. Their daughter, Claudia Antonia, was but a year old, and she would remain with her father, further adding to Aelia's grief. Claudius, who adored his wife and was dismayed at having to abandon her, had at least shown great courage in gaining the assurance of the Emperor that her life would be spared. In light of the ongoing tragedies that continued to fester, he took what little solace he could in that at least Tiberius had kept that promise.

# Chapter XVIII: Festival of Sorrow

*20 December, 31 A.D.*

\*\*\*

*Claudius*

Saturnalia had come to Rome, and all tried their best to put the dark events of the past few months behind them in the revelry and drunken celebrations. The famous poet, Catullus, a century before had called it "the best of days". And yet, during this usually joyous time, a dark cloud hung stubbornly over Rome.

Proculus had elected to take a leave of absence from Rome. He owned a very respectable estate in Gaul that his wife, Vorena, had inherited many years before. Calvinus and his wife were spending the holiday with their daughter's family in Neapolis. Draco was a widower, with his only son serving as a legionary in Hispania. As such, he had decided to spend Saturnalia at the imperial palace, under his disguise of a slave, "To see how generous the imperial house really is".

With most of their friends away for the holiday, Cursor had sought to clear his mind and soul by writing an unusual letter of sorts. He viewed it as his confession for his part in the terrible calamities of the past year. It was not addressed to anyone in Rome, or to his peers who served on the Rhine, but to an old friend who was posted in the east. Artorius was a Centurion Pilus Prior and commander of the First Italic Cohort in Judea. An unusual amalgamation, the cohort consisted of volunteers from various legions around the Empire and was a completely independent entity, answering only to the governor, Pontius Pilate. Pilate had been a close confidant of Sejanus, who had acted as his benefactor. Yet for reasons few understood, Pilate had somehow escaped the wrath of Tiberius during the bitter purge that followed Sejanus' fall. Cursor had not seen Artorius since his own departure from the Rhine, though he tried to keep abreast as to how his friend was faring in the east.

Though Cursor did consider Pontius Pilate both a friend and equal, he was not sure what his reaction would be if he learned that Cursor had been instrumental in his patron's destruction. Because of this, he decided to pen his confession to Artorius. Unless an unforeseen disaster toppled him politically, the Centurion Pilus Prior was almost assured elevation into the Equites once he decided to leave the legions behind him. Therefore, Cursor felt it appropriate to address him as an equal in their correspondence. And if Artorius decided to let Pilate know that Cursor had played a substantial part in Sejanus' fall, so be it. The possibility of losing Pilate's friendship was a risk Cursor was willing to accept in order to purge the guilt that wracked his spirit.

As he finished the letter to his friend in the east, Adela entered, bearing a message for him. Her face was ashen and he surmised that the news she brought was bleak. It was a short note from Cassius Chaerea, confirming Cursor's worst fears regarding Sejanus' children.

"I must go," he said quietly.

"You cannot save them if the order came from Tiberius," Adela replied.

"I brought this about, and I must see it through to its conclusion. Think of it as my penance for my role in this dark saga."

"I love you," Adela said, giving his hand a reassuring squeeze as tears welled up in her eyes.

The final act of repugnant vengeance made ready to play out. Though Claudius was able to save his former wife, there was to be no hope for Sejanus' remaining children. Aelianus was but thirteen, his sister, Junilla, a year younger. Dusk had fallen, and as they were escorted to the top of the Gemonian Stairs, there were no crowds to greet their downfall. Whatever the people had thought of Sejanus, they found the killing of his underage children repugnant, and therefore the forum was almost completely deserted.

Cursor watched the proceedings from the overhanging façade at the Temple of Concord. Aelianus was dressed in his formal toga, signifying him to be a grown man. The Tribune reasoned it was probably how they justified his execution. The boy tried to keep a brave face as the rope was placed around his neck. His eyes grew wide in panic, the cord quickly tightening, choking off his screams. The executioner maintained the constricting binds for far longer than they had with the boy's father, as there was no crowd to finish him off. It took some time, with his head turning purple and then blue as the circulation was cut off and he slowly asphyxiated. Once satisfied that the task was complete, the body was thrown down the stairs, where is lay in a twisted heap.

It was when the young girl was brought forward that the horrid scene degraded even further. Cursor could hear her screaming loudly and there was a great commotion from amongst the Praetorians surrounding her. One of their Centurions was quickly walking towards the Tribune, hand over his mouth and eyes clenched shut.

"What's happening?" Cursor asked, grabbing the man by the shoulder.

"Well sir," the Centurion began, swallowing hard. "The thing is, there is no precedent for the execution of a virgin. So…"

*"No!"* Cursor shouted, realizing what the Praetorians were doing to the poor girl. As he started towards the execution square, the Centurion grabbed him by his toga.

"Don't try to stop them, sir," he said quickly; his words drowned out by the girl's shrieks of pain and terror. "It is the only way to make this legal."

"They are children!" Cursor emphasized, his face red with anger and sorrow. "They were guiltless of any crime; there is *nothing* legal about this!" He shook off the Centurion's grip, and unable to take the horrid spectacle anymore, quickly walked off in the opposite direction. The girl's screams as she was defiled, even while the rope was placed around her neck, would haunt the Tribune for the remainder of his days.

As he made his way through the forum, his eyes wet with tears, he was approached by the only welcome sight on that horrifying evening. It was Claudius, and at first the Tribune wondered what he was doing there. He then remembered that Aelianus and Junilla had been his nephew and niece. Cursor placed a hand on his shoulder, his face wrought with emotion.

"I...I tried to save them," Claudius said as his voice choked up. "I went to Capri once more, yet was not allowed anywhere near my uncle. Those Praetorian b...bastards said he wasn't well and did not wish to see anyone." He ran his hand over his eyes, unable to fight back his falling tears.

"What have we done?" Cursor asked in exasperation, thankful that the condemned girl's crying had finally ceased.

"T...this was not your doing," Claudius said, nodding his head towards the Gemonian Stairs across the forum. "You did your duty and brought down a traitor; this v...vile act was sanctioned by others."

Cursor's eyes fell and he found his breathing was ragged.

"We shoulder much, but do not take on ourselves the evils committed by others," he said quietly, quoting his wife as he tried to compose himself.

"I'm sorry?" Claudius asked, puzzled as he did not hear him. The Tribune simply shook his head.

"This is not what I fought for," Cursor stated, regaining his demeanor. "I did not spend twenty years fighting the Empire's wars on the frontier, nor did I risk everything in exposing a potential usurper just so I could watch children being raped and executed for their father's crimes."

"You did what you knew to be right," Claudius reassured him. "What else could you have done?"

"And you have lost so much; your sister, your wife, your niece and nephews. What do you have left?"

"Livilla was her own downfall," Claudius said, shaking his head. "M...my life has consisted of one great loss after another. Aelia lives, gods be thanked, and she knows that I still love her. And I do have my daughter. W…we cannot hold ourselves accountable for the evil of others. This shadow will pass my friend, and perhaps one day we will find Rome worthy of serving once more."

It was the strangest thing; for all of his involvement in the fall of Sejanus, few if anyone even mentioned Tribune Aulus Nautius Cursor when discussing it. It was as if he had never been a part of the harrowing saga at all. Of course after the Senate issued its decree of *Damnatio Memoriae*, in essence wiping out the existence of Lucius Aelius Sejanus, it stood to reason that little emphasis would be given to those who brought him down. Many expected a similar decree of damnation would be passed on Livilla after the Senate reconvened after the start of the year. Cursor counted himself fortunate that whatever the histories said about the fall of Sejanus, his own part in the hated affair would be forgotten by posterity. It was a strange thing, that he had been instrumental in a number of historic affairs, yet few if any would remember his name after he was gone. Being consigned to the anonymity of the history suited him just fine.

Cursor watched as Claudius limped away from the Forum, his words playing over in his mind. He next looked back towards the Gemonian Stairs, thankful that in the engulfing night he could not see the bodies of the two young children that lay twisted on the steps. He then thought about his own words he'd spoken once; that duty and the love of his wife were the only things he was certain of. After what he had just witnessed, he found that 'duty' was now a hollow term to him.

What Cursor could not know was that in years to come the verses of the divine Sybil, who had foreseen Claudius as "the savior or Rome", would come to fruition. His humane kindness, as well as his impeccable sense of duty and valor, would be remembered. And under Emperor Claudius Caesar, Tribune Aulus Nautius Cursor would embark on one final campaign, where he would find Rome worthy of serving once more.

19274403R00082

Printed in Poland
by Amazon Fulfillment
Poland Sp. z o.o., Wrocław